BLESSED BE THE WICKED

KEL CARPENTER

Blessed Be the Wicked

Published by Kel Carpenter

Copyright © 2019, Kel Carpenter LLC

Contributions made by Lucinda Dark

Edited by Analisa Denny

Proofread by Dominique Laura

Cover Art by Trif

Map and Graphic Designed by Zenta Brice

 Created with Vellum

Chaos isn't a pit. Chaos is a ladder. Many who try to climb it fail, and never get to try again. The fall breaks them. And some are given a chance to climb, but refuse. They cling to the realm, or love, or the gods . . . illusions. Only the ladder is real. The climb is all there is. But they'll never know this. Not until it's too late.

~ Littlefinger, *Game of Thrones*, Season 3, Episode 6

The Sirian Continent

THE CRYSTAL CONTINENT

TRITOL

LIPH

N'SKARA

JIBREAL

ILVAS

VUSUT

CISEA

CISEAN MOUNTAINS

B A N G R A T A S

DUMAS

ZYBURN

NORCASTA

SARI SARI ISLANDS

T R I E N E

LEONE

IAMONT

The Pirate Queen

"All queens are pirates in their own time."
— Quinn Darkova, vassal of House Fierté, fear twister

G old. It glittered at every turn. Quinn wasn't
sure what to expect in the infamous city of
Tritol, but true to the Pirate Queen's name, it was a
city of fortune.

Burnished domes of yellow and bronze lit up
like beacons under the swelter of Leviticus' eye. A
hazy film obscured Quinn's vision as she squinted
through the sand being swept around as they were
urged through the gates of the main plaza. Textiles

in every color hung from windows and doorways as shopkeepers opened for the day.

She'd heard the rumors that Imogen liked her people to display affluence and looked favorably upon it. If the overly friendly merchants were anything to go by, Quinn was inclined to believe those rumors as they offered gifts and trinkets to the girl who went before them, urging her horse by its reins.

"For the Queen!" they proclaimed, holding out their best fabrics and golden treasures. Axe simply shook her head and held up a hand, brushing them off with ease as she rode down the sandy streets as if she owned them. If she truly was Imogen's adoptive daughter—one day she might.

"You know," Quinn started, glancing over at Lazarus, "you could really learn a thing or two here." She gestured to a vendor, and they jumped forward, offering up a necklace made of several ropes of gold. The man bowed his head, lifting it up, and just as Quinn leaned over to accept it, Lazarus cast her a disapproving glance.

"It's not for you," he said.

Quinn narrowed her eyes but took her hand back without the necklace and didn't say anything more as they moved farther into the city.

The heat bore down on them. The open air growing more humid the longer they walked. Quinn glanced from side to side and then focused straight ahead, keeping her eyes on the strange girl that led them.

Axe continued to ignore the offerings of the citizens of Tritol as she led their party toward the tallest building in the city. It jutted out from the rest of the capital. The sharp edge of its tip glimmering under the sunlight. *More gold*, Quinn affirmed.

She whistled beneath her breath as they arrived at the gates of the building—tall arches were encrusted with jewels in sapphire blue and royal purple. Sea creatures of myth and legend had been carved into the stone itself. Mermaids. Krakens. Creatures from the deep blue that had been rumored to be the goddess Myori in years past.

Only sunken ships and sailors at the bottom of the ocean could really say.

"No wonder we curse her wrath," Quinn murmured. Lazarus shot her another look. One that she ignored.

The gates lifted when Axe raised her hand to the men at the top. Just inside, they all came to a halt in the center of a blooming courtyard.

Towering trees dangled wisteria over the area; vines crept up the stone walls.

"Alright," Axe announced. "She's expectin' us."

Quinn handed the reins to an approaching stable boy, then turned and followed the others. She took an appreciative glance of the glittering gold-encrusted moldings on the walls as they entered the building. The floor was made of wide pearl bricks and cream mortar that was stained reddish-brown in sections. *Blood*, she surmised, having seen the signs before in another country. Another time.

Axe bounded up a set of stairs leading to a chamber littered with pillows of the highest quality. An older woman with olive skin and harsh features lounged on top of a golden claw-foot chair. Her dark hair, streaked with gray, was braided tightly, outlining the sharp bones of her face. A lone scar curved down her cheek, running parallel to her jawline. A billowing white shirt slid from one shoulder to reveal strange black markings on her skin. Symbols of pirates. She must be their queen.

"*Madara*, I'm home!" Axe announced cheerfully as she rushed to greet the woman.

The woman's eyes opened slowly, and she turned her head toward the newcomers—her pale lips curled into a brutal smile as she sat up.

"Yes," she said. "And it looks like you've brought"—she paused, crinkling her nose in distaste—"uninvited guests."

Axe grinned happily and plopped herself on the hard arm of the chair. "Just as you asked," she said. "They've got quite the party too."

"Do they?" The Queen said, taking them in.

Axe flashed her a bright smile and winked. Quinn blinked at the odd girl, not sure what to make of her.

"Lazarus Fierté," Imogen started, pulling at Quinn's attention. "Thorne of the mountains sent a hawk informing us of your impending arrival. We expected you, but not quite this soon."

Lazarus stepped forward, crossing an arm over his chest, his hand over his heart.

"Queen Imogen," he said with a respectful nod, before lowering his arm. "Yes, I'm afraid we had to move the timeline of our arrival."

"I can see that." Imogen tilted her head to the side and said nothing more as she waited.

"Thank you for allowing me an audience on such short notice. I know it is customary to request one in advance," Lazarus continued, his voice exceedingly persuasive. The man could make a woman drink poison from his palm with a smile. Quinn admired that about him.

It took a certain ruthlessness to befriend an enemy and kill them with a grin.

Imogen sighed and crossed one leg over the other, her pale shirt bunching against the pile of cushions at her back. To the side, Axe smirked and watched the proceedings with curiosity. Quinn narrowed her eyes on the girl as Lazarus spoke once more.

"I'd like to request a private audience," he said. "As the future king of Norcasta, it would be more prudent to discuss my proposal in a more . . ." Lazarus paused, scanning the throne room pointedly before finishing, "secluded setting."

The Queen sighed and leaned her head back as if already tired of his presence. She flitted her attention from Lazarus to Draeven and onto Vaughn, where her only reaction was a slight narrowing of eyes, before settling on Quinn. Quinn stared back unflinching, regardless of propriety.

She could almost hear Lorraine's terse voice telling her to mind her manners and show respect. Instead of annoying her, a sliver of worry crept inside as she thought about where Lorraine might be right now, and in what condition.

Quinn's expression hardened with resolve, knowing that concern was for another time.

"Rather than your proposal," Imogen said, "I'd like to know why there are several dozen men dressed in Ilvan colors lying dead just outside my city."

"*Madara*—" Axe began, the girl's eyes shooting to her mother's with slight befuddlement.

Imogen raised her hand, stilling any further words from Axe. "Now, now, *Tesora*, let them answer my question."

Axe frowned but backed off, and Quinn noted the interaction with interest.

"As heir to the Norcastan throne, I have made quite a few enemies for myself and my vassals," Lazarus answered. "I apologize for the inconvenience, and I can assure you that the men lying dead outside these walls are no citizens of yours. They are nothing but mercenaries—hired to dispatch me and my party."

"Hmmmm." Quinn did not like the way the woman hummed. It was far too condescending for the alliance Lazarus wished to broker. "Yes, I have heard that Claudius had a new heir," she said lightly. With a wave of her palm, she gestured for one of the servants standing to the side. The man stepped forward and held out a challis that she took from him. Drinking deep from the cup, Imogen sighed and licked the wine stain from her lips. "So," she continued. "That must make you the dark prince?"

Quinn frowned. Lazarus' lack of response, however, didn't deter the Pirate Queen. She held her challis out and stared down at him. "As the dark prince," she said, "you mean to tell me that you led criminals—imposters—to *my* doorstep?"

"They have been taken care of," Lazarus replied.

Quinn recalled how vividly they'd been dealt with. She'd never forget the sounds of their bones snapping and their screams echoing out into the void. Something had changed in her that moment.

Because she'd never be able to go back now that she knew how much she craved it.

"Nevertheless," Imogen said, "involving me and my people in your petty Norcastan squabbles before you have even been granted an audience is a serious offense, Lord Fierté." Her voice came out hard and biting, a clear warning that she was not to be trifled with.

"They are—" he began, thunder lacing his voice.

"Oh, I know what the squabble was about," she said coolly. "You do not become the Pirate Queen —recognized and feared throughout the land and sea—without learning to read the waves of people as well. I know all about your *enemies*, Lazarus Fierté, just as I know you may be the heir to Norcasta, but you are not the *blood heir*." She raised a brow again, silencing Lazarus where he stood.

Axe yawned, swinging her arms just enough to sway them around her sides—the picture of a bored child. Draeven clenched his jaw in a silent fury. His knuckles whitened. But Quinn knew this rage was not truly from their current situation and was instead the fervor that had been inside her—now taken into him. She still couldn't believe that Draeven—obnoxious Lord Sunshine—was a rage thief.

Then again, she'd seen stranger in her time. *She* was stranger.

Despite the waves of tension that wafted from his left-hand, and all that rage just waiting to be released again, Lazarus remained stoic and composed. "Then perhaps you understand my reason for requesting an audience with you, Queen Imogen," he said.

Before the woman could respond, the great hall

doors opened, and echoing footsteps approached from behind. Quinn turned back as a new man entered. The guards bowed low.

Tall and slender, he dressed in black garb with only a white and blue tie around his waist. The colored ends dangled to the man's feet. Quinn watched him as he moved to step around their group and toward Queen Imogen with a familiarity that belied his lack of courtly attire.

"You're late," Axe said absently.

The man didn't respond as he bowed low over the Queen's feet. "I do apologize for my tardiness," he said. "I was not informed that your guests had arrived."

Imogen sighed and flicked her fingers at the man. "No matter," she said. "You're here now."

He rose to his feet and bowed once more, taking the Queen's hand and pressing a chaste kiss to one of the many rings on her knuckles. "Thank you, my lady."

Quinn lifted a brow as Axe's lips curled back in distaste as the man moved to stand behind the opposite side of her chair. "This is my advisor, Zorel Vordlain," Imogen said as she leaned to the side and handed her now empty cup to a servant.

"That is a Norcastan name, is it not?" Lazarus

commented, his gaze dropping down to conceal his expression.

Zorel nodded. "Yes, the Vordlains are Norcastan noblemen; lords overseeing the vast countryside," he said. "But I have lived in Ilvas for many years. It has become my home."

Lazarus' expression didn't change as he nodded. "I am Lazarus Fierté, heir to the Norcastan throne," he introduced. "These are my vassals, Draeven and Quinn." Lazarus didn't turn as he said, "And behind me is Vaughn, an emissary of Thorne, leader of the Cisean tribes."

"I see. And what business do you have here with my Queen?" Zorel inquired.

It didn't escape Quinn's notice that Axe's expression darkened on the advisor as he spoke. The Queen leaned over and whispered a hair too loud in Ilvan.

"He is the dark prince you spoke of."

The man's expression didn't shift, and Quinn didn't flinch, keeping her gaze fixed. They had to know that neither Lazarus nor Draeven spoke Ilvan. They assumed that she couldn't as well. Quinn kept her smirk to herself.

Lazarus flashed them a tight smile, barely restraining the savagery behind it. "I am here to discuss matters of great urgency between our two countries," he answered—ignoring the comment that he couldn't translate. "I think it would befit the Queen of Ilvas and the future king of Norcasta to come to an agreement that aids us both." Lazarus dismissed Zorel without another word, turning his attention back to the Queen.

Quinn coughed, trying to disguise her chuckle. Judging by Lazarus' withering glare and Axe's beaming smile, she did a poor job of it.

"Your Highness," Lazarus continued, "I have an alliance with the Cisean tribes, and I intend to broker a similar arrangement with N'skara. Would you not want to be included in such an alliance—when your country borders all three?"

Quinn's body went still as those words sunk in.

N'skara.

Her homeland.

Her kinsmen.

Lazarus had no idea the thoughts his words just spawned. Nor did he understand that his actions might have very different consequences than the ones he intended. Quinn kept those feelings hidden, instead focusing on the conversation before her and the way Imogen's eyes fell on her.

The Queen pursed her lips, fighting a smile as

she continued. "A vassal that hails from those pale prudes, but not an emissary. Do you pay her handsomely for her disloyalty to her own people?"

"My loyalty can't be bought," Quinn said, stepping forward to answer for herself. "I am loyal to those who are loyal to me. Lazarus has so far proven himself as a worthy man to follow, and my homeland has *nothing* to do with my attachment to him." She discreetly skipped over the contract she'd agreed to, gambling her life as payment.

Imogen stood and descended from her throne with the swagger of a true pirate. "Loyalty is important to you, then?" she asked, walking around Quinn in circles to take her in.

Quinn stared forward, unflinching as she said, "Survival is important to me. Having dependable friends in high places makes that easier."

Imogen's lips quirked up. "I like you," she stated. "You don't mince your words."

"Loyalty, much like family, is not always decided by blood." Quinn flicked her gaze to the red-haired girl, and Imogen blinked, her attention sharpening. "They are my people."

"So I see." With a nod of begrudging respect, the Pirate Queen turned back toward her throne. As she ascended the dais, she spoke. "Zorel, you will escort Lord Fierté and his vassals, as well as the emissary, to their quarters. They may stay under my roof for the time being. It is the season for cheer, after all. The holiday will be starting soon."

Zorel bowed low and then began to make his way down the steps and toward their group. Lazarus stepped to the side as Zorel approached, blocking his view. "About our audience—" he started.

Imogen waved him off. "Another time, Lord Fierté," she said. "As you pointed out, requests for audiences—especially *private* audiences—must be made in advance." Imogen turned with flare, sitting back upon her throne and crossing her legs with a haughty glance in his direction. "Or was there another reason you wanted to speak with me in private? Perhaps an intimate proposal of some sort?"

Quinn scowled at the insinuation, stepping forward as Zorel came to a stop at the end of the stairs. Lazarus put his hand on her arm to stop her, and he shook his head. "No, Your Highness." Then he bowed low as Quinn's upper lip curled back slightly. Axe grinned, leaning to the side as she propped her arm up on the chair and placed her chin on her upturned palm. "I would simply request that we speak at your earliest convenience."

Imogen nodded. "After the festivities then. Do enjoy yourselves."

Lazarus bowed and turned to follow as Zorel gestured for them to depart. As they left, Quinn glanced over her shoulder at the two women who watched them. Axe waved with a smile while the Pirate Queen of Ilvas merely smirked, a gleam of villainous joy in her eye.

Inquisition

"Curiosity is the bane of secrets."
— *Quinn Darkova, vassal of House Fierté, fear twister*

Q uinn lifted her fist and let it fall against the heavy wooden door.

Footsteps sounded before the handle turned and metal creaked as the door opened and a stout woman with salt-and-pepper hair peered out. Her already thin lips pressed together as her eyes narrowed in suspicion. Behind the woman lay a familiar figure.

"I'm here for Lorraine," Quinn said. When the

healer woman stared up at her unblinking, Quinn frowned. "I'm a . . . I'm a friend," she settled on eventually with a tight smile. "Of hers—the healer," she added, nodding toward the prone woman. "We came to the city together," she continued. "Lord Fierté said he'd given permission for me to see her . . ."

The healer sighed in exasperation and asked in Ilvan, "Are you with the party that brought her?"

Quinn opened her mouth to respond and paused, realizing the woman couldn't understand Norcastan. That was why she had been blankly staring at her. Quinn wasn't sure if she wanted to play her hand just yet and reveal her knowledge of their language. It had been over a day since they'd arrived in Ilvas, and Lazarus said Lorraine was only *just* out of the woods. Dominicus hadn't wanted to allow her back so soon, but after much deliberation, Quinn was permitted to visit Lorraine so long as she didn't disturb her.

Whatever that means.

She opened her mouth to reply to the healer when another voice spoke. "Aye, she's with the group," Axe said in Ilvan, strolling down the hall. Small axes were strapped to either side of her hips, and their handles swung with each exaggerated step she took. The girl was too old to be truly considered a child, but too young to be a true woman. Even so, she was small for her age; her stature slight.

The healer nodded and stepped back, holding the door open for Quinn to pass through.

Quinn stalled for a minute before flicking a glance back at Axe and nodding to her. "Thank you for that."

"'Course." Axe shrugged with a small grin, gesturing toward the open doorway. "After you."

Quinn frowned at the motion, wondering why the girl was here but continued forward anyways. The pale-faced woman in bed drew her attention.

Lorraine looked strange—devoid of her natural vitality. She had been shot through the back when Quinn had freed the basilisk during the battle. An unknown feeling dug at Quinn's insides. She had wanted to scare the enemy. She'd wanted to see them flee from Neiss, only to be killed. She hadn't the forethought in that moment to realize that everyone considered Neiss a threat—even those horses carrying the very people she meant to protect. It was Lorraine that was left wide open and unprotected when the archers had taken aim. The beasts only knew fear, and her mistake had almost cost Lorraine her life. Quinn clenched her fists as she looked down at one of the only people who had given a damn about her and her future.

She didn't understand the foreign emotion invading her, making her chest tighten every time she replayed the events in her mind. If she could change the actions she had taken in that battle, she would. She would have brought forth her creatures of fear at the first sign of an attack. She would have slaughtered them. She would have stopped this from ever happening. She would have—

"You alright there?" Axe spoke up from behind her.

Quinn stilled, swallowing down the thickness in her throat. She cleared it once and said, "I'm fine."

The younger woman tsked and walked around her to take the only vacant seat at the end of the bed. She plopped down and sprawled her legs, not bothering to cross them as a princess might. "You look guilty."

Quinn blanched. "What did you say?"

"I said, you look guilty," she repeated. Axe thrust her chin toward Quinn. "Your hands are clenched. You're scowlin'—and it's not very pretty, if you must know—"

"Do you have a point?" Quinn deadpanned.

The girl sucked the air between her teeth obnoxiously.

"No point." Axe shook her head.

Quinn's scowl deepened as she turned away and took a seat on the edge of the bed. She grasped Lorraine's clammy fingers between her own and squeezed gently.

"Actually," she started again. Quinn let out a growl as the girl continued on, "I do have a question."

"And what makes you think you're entitled to answers?" Quinn replied stiffly.

Axe went quiet, and just when Quinn thought she wasn't going to respond at all she said, "Nothin', but what's the harm in askin'? You learn a great deal just by takin' chances. Never know what people are willin' to part with . . ."

Gods above. She was worse than Draeven and just as manipulative as Lazarus, but not quite as skilled. *Yet.* She was far too honest to be as competent as the man Quinn served.

"Nothing. So if you're done trying to pry, I'm trying to help her," Quinn growled, turning back to the sleeping woman.

"Are you a healer?" Axe asked, completely ignoring what she just said.

"No."

"Then how can you help her?"

Quinn was half a second from ripping into the girl when Lorraine shifted. The movement drew her attention as a weak moan escaped her fellow vassal's lips. Quinn frowned, not sure what to do as the healer came beside her and motioned for Quinn to move.

"Up! Up!" the woman snapped in Ilvan.

Quinn stood and frowned as the old woman pushed the blankets aside. Beneath the heavy fabric, Lorraine was naked and shivering. Bandages and bloodied cloth covered most of her stomach. Strips of material had been tied at her sides to hold both dressings together, the one on her back where the arrow had first pierced and the one on her front where it broke the skin again.

The healer inhaled sharply as she shifted the pieces of cloth aside to reveal the wound itself. The hole had been stitched closed with thread, but a reddish-brown crust of dried blood rimmed the edges of the wound, and when Lorraine moved again, a drop of fresh crimson welled up.

The woman let out a curse and motioned to Quinn. "Me?"

"No—the tonic," she replied in terse Ilvan.

Quinn was already turning when Axe translated it. On the short table behind her sat various jars of colored liquids and powders, clean dressings, thread, and scissors. There were other implements there too, ones that Quinn might have been fascinated by were they not being used on Lorraine. She swept her eyes over the assortment when a plump arm reached around her and grasped a small stone bowl with a green solution that glowed faintly.

The healer tsked, pushing Quinn aside with her rump to come kneel by the bed. She put the bowl to Lorraine's cracked lips and guided her head up at an angle. The healer tilted the bowl, and the green substance poured into her mouth. Unconscious, Lorraine rejected it at first, coughing as the tonic slid down her throat. The process lasted several minutes, and throughout it all, Quinn watched at a loss.

She glanced over at Axe, but the girl only shrugged, leaning forward to rest her elbows on her knees. "Don't take it too personal. Harrietta is a great healer, but her table manners are atrocious." She shook her head and the beads in her hair clinked together.

"Yeah, well, she's not alone," Quinn answered pointedly.

Axe leaned back and put a hand to her chest, mock offended. "I'm not the one that put her in that bed," she defended herself. Quinn grit her teeth, but the girl's next words stopped her cold. "Do your veins always turn black when you're annoyed?"

She glanced down at herself, and indeed, it was as Axe said. The veins of her arms had run dark, black wisps drifting from her skin. Quinn took a slow, steady breath, and instead of responding, she whispered, "I'll be back," before turning on her heel. She thrust the door open and was halfway down the hallway before she heard the door close a second time.

"Wait!" Axe called out, jogging after her. She stopped a few feet away, letting her boots slip a bit on the polished floors, gliding until she came to a stop about a foot or so away.

"What do you want?" Quinn asked, wondering if she was in Fortuna's good graces right now or if asking a favor, like Axe leaving her be, would land her with a spree of bad luck. She couldn't exactly afford the latter.

"I'm curious about you," the pirate princess said, blowing a lock of shiny red hair out of her face. "You're kind of rude, and you got the black magic thin' goin' on—"

"You can see my magic?" Quinn interrupted, turning to face her fully. "How?" she demanded.

Axe shrugged. "Gift from a goddess."

Quinn stared at her impassively. "What kind of Maji are you?" she asked, narrowing her eyes.

"Not a Maji," the girl answered with a smile. It was completely genuine, which perplexed her all the more.

"Skeevs can't see magic," Quinn replied.

"Oy! Just 'cause I'm not a black magic hussy doesn't mean you got to be mean now."

Quinn gritted her teeth. "If you're not a Maji, then you have no magic of your own—"

"I told you, it was a gift from a goddess," the younger girl repeated. Quinn rolled her eyes and started back down the hallway. "Hey—where are you goin'?"

"Back to my room."

"But what about my question?" the girl called after her, jogging to keep up with Quinn's much longer legs.

Quinn's eyes rolled skywards once more. Fortuna had to be messing with her, but it was never a good day when she became entertainment for the gods. "What about it?"

Small, sticky fingers wrapped around her wrist, attempting to pull her to a halt. Quinn stopped. The girl was old enough to know better and act as a lady, as Lorraine might call it, yet she didn't. She appeared to be about fifteen but still acted as a child, and if she kept at it, that was what Quinn would call her. "I've only seen N'skari from afar when they send messengers to talk with *Madara,* and they're all a bunch of limp seaweed stalks—" Quinn hunched over, coughing hoarsely and laughing at the same time. The pirate princess wasn't wrong. In her opinion, at least. "Are you okay?"

"Fine," Quinn answered, clearing her throat.

"So anyways—you're not like them—and not just because you got some weird magic. You act different. How'd you end up with Lord Fierté in Norcasta? So far as I know, N'skari keep to themselves. Bunch of superior pricks, they are."

Quinn stood there, knowing that if she walked away without answering, the girl would follow. She sighed, exhaling a heavy breath before speaking. "He saved me from the noose the day I was supposed to hang."

"And you're indebted to him?" Axe pressed.

"Something like that." Quinn quickly withdrew her arm from the girl and turned, heading down the hall.

Tensions Rising

"No one is truly infallible."
— Lazarus Fierté, soul eater, heir to Norcasta, sullen prince

L azarus sipped from the decanter of amber fluid in his hand. The firewater slid down his throat as he clenched his jaw and stared out from the balcony, over the sea of luxury that was Tritol. His quarters allowed them a view of the city, as well as a now half-empty stock of spirits.

"So, what are we doing here?" Draeven had tempered some of the fury eating at him since their arrival by practicing his swordsmanship with the Queen's guard. Judging by the lack of bruises or cuts, Lazarus assumed he'd done well, though he didn't ask. His left-hand stepped up alongside him to take in the view. "The Queen's not willing to speak with you until after her holiday. Are we staying for that?"

Lazarus swallowed back the rest of his alcohol and set the glass to the side. "I don't have much of a choice, do I?" He sighed, closing his eyes and brushing his calloused hand over his jaw, scraping against the stubble there. "I'm not willing to leave Ilvas without an alliance with Imogen, or at least the knowledge of where she stands. If I have to wait her out for a week, so be it."

Dominicus stepped up behind them. "And Lorraine?" His weapons master inquired.

Lazarus nodded. "She'll need time to recover, even with the tonics and the healer Maji at work."

"You have plan?" Behind the three of them, Vaughn splayed himself out on a lounge, spinning a rustic knife between his scarred fingers. The mountain man was pale, but the lines crossing his fingers and palms were stark—a true white the color of bone. They were the hands of a man that had trained with weapons and knives all his life, until he was no longer clumsy enough to cut himself.

Lazarus handed his empty glass to Dominicus

before leveling a look at the Cisean. "Of course, I have a plan," he replied. "We'll stay in Ilvas for the next week, till the holiday ends and the Queen grants me my audience."

"The Queen be beautiful woman . . ."

Lazarus did not appreciate the implication in the Cisean's voice. "Recall that you are only here as a dog to your master, boy," he said sharply. "You are an emissary. Nothing more." He may have understood the necessity of Thorne's friendship, and while he tolerated the puppy that wagged his tail at Quinn, he did not like the mountain boy that followed her around. He made that known, and yet, Vaughn merely smirked at him as if he knew exactly what was going on in Lazarus' head.

But no one really knew just how twisted both he and the voices had become.

Being near her had been torture; but kissing her —having her—and then trying to pull away again . . . that was a misery in and of itself. Quinn was the forbidden fruit—clever and forceful in her temptation—and he was the future king that desired her *almost* as much as his crown.

But not quite.

He couldn't afford the complications of her, and yet, he couldn't stand the way the mongrel stared at her, talked to her, sparred with her. They'd gotten close in these past weeks, and he despised it.

"Lazarus," Draeven said, capturing his attention once more. "We'll need to stay for longer than a week. Lorraine might be stitched up, but she won't be able to ride on horseback for a good while longer. That will create complications in getting to N'skara."

Dominicus refilled the glass Lazarus had given him and handed it over as they all moved back into the room. Draeven shut the doors behind them and took his position on a lounge opposite of Vaughn. Lazarus tipped his glass up and swallowed half the contents in one gulp.

"You're right," he said. "At the very least, it seems we'll be here for two weeks. Imogen will not be as easily won as Thorne. She doesn't appreciate other people stepping on her territory as we had to upon our arrival. It would be different if she were in the thick of it and we came to help, but where it stands, Imogen is a prideful woman with every reason to be."

"What makes you say that?" Draeven asked.

"Which part?"

"All of it," Dominicus answered for him.

Lazarus nodded, stroking the stubble along his jaw for a moment.

Lazarus strode toward the windows, the dark blue skyline attracting his gaze while the lights of torches flickered in the distance. "Do you know what this holiday is about?" he asked.

No one answered. "Imogen, the infamous Pirate Queen, captured Tritol —this city—and then the remaining cities of Ilvas ten years ago this week. She united the city states of the Republic of Ilvas and brought them all under one reign. She gave them peace and prosperity. She's a Queen made, not born—and in order to accomplish all of that, no man or woman could do so unless they had pride in spades. We killed on her soil without her army or her permission, and so, she's punishing me with the wait to remind me of my place," Lazarus explained, taking another sip. The burn lulled the voices into greater submission, at least for the time being. He turned back to the room.

"You think she's upset because she wasn't involved?" Dominicus asked, grimacing with uncertainty. The man operated with logic, not heart, and that wouldn't help him understand this enemy.

"I know it. She enjoys nothing more than a good fight." Lazarus shook his head, remembering the first time they'd met, nearly fifteen years ago. "Though, she does play the part of a court politician well. I'm surprised her daughter is not as adept."

"Axe?" Draeven lifted a brow.

Lazarus nodded, gesturing absently with his free hand. "The girl is reckless. Like Imogen in her youth. More so, even."

"She's still a child," Draeven pointed out.

"A child with the keys to a kingdom that her mother fought to earn. I wonder if she will temper with age, as her mother seems to have," Lazarus mused. When he'd first met the Queen, she was only a woman in her prime. A pirate still, but a woman, nevertheless. The girl wasn't yet there, but she wasn't that far off either.

"You sound as though you know Imogen quite well. You've met her before?" Draeven asked, narrowing his eyes.

Lazarus sighed heavily. "Once, and it was before you and I met. She was only a captain then, not a Queen. She ransacked the city of Iamont and stole from that king's coffers. A group of bandits helped her escape, and in return, she gave the people half the riches she took."

"Beautiful and fierce . . ." Vaughn said as he

stood from his seated position and ambled over to the decanter of spirits, or what remained of it. "She and she-wolf Quinn are same."

Draeven let out a choked cough as Lazarus sent him a withering glare. "Her actions led to the collapse of the monarchy and the eventual rise of the current empire. An empire that has been very fortuitous in their affairs with Ilvas. Imogen may be a queen of the people, but she is also a manipulative woman who will fight with words as much as swords."

"Combat and politics are not so dissimilar," Draeven said after his coughing died down. "They're both held on a battlefield, just different kinds. If Imogen is a fighter at heart, then she understands the best way to win a fight is to watch your enemy. If you understand them, then you understand how they will respond." Vaughn selected a glass and poured himself a healthy amount of the same amber fluid Lazarus was drinking. Draeven continued, "Maybe you're right and she was angry that she wasn't notified. If she didn't know, then she wasn't watching, and that makes this a greater gamble to her. She's forcing us to sit this out so she can watch."

Perhaps, Lazarus thought. *Or perhaps, she was*

merely pretending to have no information. He was no fool. He had noticed the way Quinn's eyes had narrowed on the Queen and her advisor, Zorel, when they had begun speaking in Ilvan. He did, however, agree that she was stalling them to watch their movements.

"She will likely put us off a few days after the holiday is concluded," Lazarus continued. "If only to showcase her authority."

"Like two *kuras* fighting for dominance," Vaughn commented lightly. He grinned as if seeing the mountain beasts in his mind's eye. Kuras were a pack animal, not dissimilar to wolves—if you overlooked that they were twice their size and coated in feathers instead of fur. Not many of the surrounding kingdoms knew of them because they rarely wandered down into the flatlands, instead preferring the caves and the cold.

Lazarus had encountered one once. He'd barely made it out alive.

Now the beast writhed beneath his skin— trapped until the dark realm claimed them both.

Lazarus shook his head as Dominicus stepped around and faced him. "And what if Lorraine isn't healed by the time those two weeks are up?"

"We'll re-evaluate," Lazarus assured him. "She has the best care Ilvas can offer."

"Her wound may heal enough for her to travel short distances, but she would not be able to ride a horse for long periods of time," Dominicus continued, and Lazarus knew he wouldn't settle until he had an answer.

He wasn't wrong about how long it would take for her to ride comfortably, even with the best work of a healer Maji. A wound that deep—cut straight through her middle—would likely sting and pull, wearing her down by the hour. That was assuming nothing reopened and they weren't attacked along the way. Lazarus shook his head. They needed Lorraine, even apart from the fact that she had captured Dominicus' attention. If Lazarus wanted to keep the weapons master content, he would need to be careful with her recovery.

"If Lorraine is not up to long travels on horseback," Lazarus finally spoke, "then we will take a ship up the coast to N'skara. But we cannot stay here for much longer than two weeks. Time is not working alongside us as it is."

"Why is that?" Vaughn asked.

Lazarus shook his head in response. The Cisean did not need to know the extent of Claudius' illness.

"There is something else we should discuss," Draeven started slowly. Lazarus knew where it was going before Draeven was able to continue. "Quinn's wrath in that battle was stronger than anything I've ever seen."

Dominicus nodded, looking considerably more unsettled with the change of topic. "She is a concern."

"She-wolf Quinn?" Vaughn tilted his head. "She-wolf strong. Built for battle. What is problem?"

"She's ascended," Draeven said. "And somehow none of us saw the signs earlier."

Lazarus had realized that. Her powers. The force of her rage and fury. The darkness that had risen from her creatures like something straight from the dark realm of Mazzulah. There was no other explanation than that she had indeed ascended.

"She will need to be trained further," Draeven continued. "She can't be allowed to roam free."

"Quinn is not a prisoner here," Lazarus shot back. "And any attempts to treat her as such will not end well, I can assure you."

"I don't mean—"

"I will speak with her," Lazarus interrupted.

"Lazarus," Dominicus said.

He held his hand up, staying his words. He spoke directly to Draeven. "You are right that her ascension changes some things—not our travels and not my plans, but—"

Draeven shook his head slightly and stood up. Vaughn put his glass down. Lazarus was not finished, and he continued on. "I will see to it that she understands the importance of this and ensure she isn't a hindrance."

"Lazarus . . ." The inflection of Draeven's voice was resigned, and that was the moment he realized the souls beneath his flesh had stirred into a frenzy. They were no longer alone.

"No need." Lazarus' shoulders stiffened as Quinn spoke from directly behind him. "*I* will be the one to ensure that I'm not a hindrance."

Lazarus turned slowly and met her eyes— eclipsed in icy anger as they were. A moment of intense silence befell them. Quinn was the first to break eye contact as she looked at each man in the room.

"Having a meeting?" She stared at him once more, lifting a brow.

No one answered for a beat. Then Lazarus stepped forward, setting his now empty glass down on a table. "We were discussing our plans for the next few weeks," he answered.

"I see." Quinn nodded. "I was not invited."

"It was—"

Quinn held up a hand, almost in the same manner as Lazarus had to Dominicus. "It doesn't matter," she said. "When you want to discuss anything, you're free to. When you want to discuss me, however . . ." She paused, her expression growing colder, harder, and more ominous as she took them in once more. Even Vaughn shifted uncomfortably. "Next time I will be included for *that* conversation, if you'd like me to remain an active participant in your plans, that is."

With that, she turned and strode from the room through the door she'd left open. That was what they were trying to tell him, but it was a poor attempt, and now he had an agitated fear twister to deal with. With a long, frustrated breath, Lazarus shoved a hand through his hair, pushing the strands back, away from his face.

"I think, if we are done now, I will go check on Lorraine once more before I head off," Dominicus said slowly, and when Lazarus didn't respond, he took that as consent and left.

Vaughn needed no excuse. He simply followed

after him, disappearing out the door, leaving Draeven and Lazarus alone together.

"That could have gone better," Draeven commented.

"I wasn't intending to talk to her tonight, but after that, I think it might be best," Lazarus said.

"Wait." Draeven moved closer and lowered his voice despite the fact that they were alone. "There was something I wanted to know," he said. "The Queen's advisor—Zorel; have you seen him before?"

Lazarus turned his head, his eyes narrowing. "Why?"

"I'm not sure," he hesitated. "But he seems familiar. I would like to keep an eye on him."

"You have my permission, but be discreet," Lazarus warned. "I don't want to give Imogen or her advisor any reason to be more suspicious of us than they already are."

Draeven nodded. "I will not draw his attention. In this, at least, having Quinn helps. Imogen and her court will be far more interested in the two of you to pay much mind to the rest of us."

Lazarus couldn't disagree there. Much to his displeasure, the Queen had already taken an interest in Quinn's heritage. He didn't think it would be long before a member of the court approached her. He only hoped she responded correctly when they did. Given how she'd just stormed out, though . . . Lazarus grimaced. "Do you think he could possibly be working with the blood heirs?"

"I don't know. But there's something there I can't place. The fact that he's from Norcasta concerns me."

Lazarus nodded. "Watch carefully, and we'll deal with it if he becomes an issue."

Draeven tilted his head in understanding and then stepped back, but Lazarus reached out and clasped him on the shoulder. "One more thing," Lazarus said, leaning inward. "How are you feeling?"

Draeven froze for a moment, his muscles tensing under Lazarus' grip. "I'm fine," he replied, trying to cut the conversation short.

"I know you've not had time to relax, but —"

Draeven shrugged him off and ambled a few steps away. "I'm handling it. I'll speak with you tomorrow."

Lazarus watched as Draeven strode away. While the man had retained his composure, there was still the worry. Quinn's rage was far stronger than anything Draeven had ever taken. Anymore and it would be too much, even for someone as skilled as his left-hand.

Which made him wonder how the woman herself could handle such darkness, unflinching as she was. Quinn wasn't invincible, nor infallible, but perhaps she'd sat with the fury so long that she no longer felt its crushing presence . . . because it was always there.

Waiting.

The Opal Room

"Get angry, but in the end—get even."
— *Quinn Darkova, vassal of House Fierté, fear twister,*
cold-blooded woman

Hindrance.

He would ensure that she was not a *hindrance.* Quinn felt the insult down in her bones as she stormed out into the streets of Tritol. Fires lit the night—torches lining the cobblestoned roads— but there was an even deeper fire within her. She didn't care where she was heading, she just knew that she needed to leave the Queen's palace before she strangled the bastard.

Quinn would have enjoyed nothing more than to find someone else to take her frustrations out on —a rough and emotionless cheap thrill—but all around her, people drank heartily, and the scent of spirits on someone's breath was the last thing she wished to smell. The holiday Imogen had spoken of was starting tonight, and unless she was going to partake in a different kind of fun, which had been expressly forbidden, Quinn was on her own.

Those same unsuspecting fools littered the streets, pouring from their homes and shopfront doorways in drunken sprawls, laughing and chortling as they staggered along with their friends and family. Music rose up into the darkened sky as bands played in the marketplace plazas and on street corners—cheerful tunes and fast-paced harmonies that enticed onlookers to grab their partners and begin to dance.

Quinn had no idea what they were celebrating, nor did she care. All she wanted was to find a way to distract herself from the indignation eating away inside her. What little patience and kindness she held was being diminished with every step she took; with every second passing, the reminder of dark needs that remained unfulfilled became more intense.

"Hey!"

Stiffening at the familiar voice, Quinn picked up the pace. *Not that kind of distraction*, she thought.

Axe wasn't giving in, picking up her pace. "Hey! Wait up!" The girl's footsteps pounded against the cobbled streets as she rushed to Quinn's stride, tilting her youthful, heart-shaped face up. "Where're you headin' to?"

"Nowhere," Quinn said quickly, walking faster.

"Wanna come with me?" Axe stumbled and nearly fell as Quinn came to an abrupt halt and turned to the young, flame-haired irritant, but before she could so much as order her away, Axe righted herself and grabbed onto Quinn's wrist. "It's not far," Axe said. "This way."

Quinn blinked as she found herself being dragged through the throng of people toward a side alley. She didn't know why she allowed herself to be led down the empty back passage onto another crowded street—and another and another —until they finally came to a less populated area of the city where the houses and shops were plainer and the streets dirtier. Children didn't play here, and women didn't walk about. The few young ones that slunk through the alleyways were gutter rats and likely thieves. Axe seemed to pay no mind as they stopped before a particularly unsavory dwelling.

Quinn coughed as a door to the *Opal Room* opened and a wave of smoke escaped. A lumbering fat man stumbled out and didn't even spare them a glance. Gaze unfocused and his ruddy cheeks glistening with sweat, he headed down the street, feet crisscrossing in front of each other as he struggled to maintain his balance.

"What is this place?" Quinn asked.

"Where I go to get away from the palace," Axe said, striding forward. "Come on, you'll like it," she said over her shoulder.

Quinn took one last glance at the street around her before following after. Inside, it was quiet, and smoke hung heavy like a fog that didn't drift or diminish. It wasn't foul smelling, but rather a sickly sweet. Patrons hung about on barstools and stained lounges, taking puffs from metal end pieces attached to cords that were adhered to ornately made glass canisters. She'd encountered pipes like this often enough to know better than to bother wafting a hand in front of her face. It would do little good to dissuade its potent effects, but the sweet-smelling scent meant it was a kinder substance. Not so strong as the spirits or herbs used to make a man feel no pain. She accepted that as she walked forward, taking a seat on a barstool in the back.

Axe sat across from her, a small table between them. Quinn raised both eyebrows, and the girl squinted back at her.

"Don't tell me you've gotten all prudish now," the young girl said. "And here I had hope for you." Axe shook her head.

Quinn wasn't amused, but she was curious, and that kept the annoyance out of her voice. "Why'd you bring me here?"

Axe snorted and lifted her hand to wave down the bartender. A woman with more gray hair than brown flipped up a section of the wooden counter and sauntered over. She wore leather trousers and a tight camisole. Bits of cloth and ties dangled around her neck, obscuring much of her chest as she approached.

"'Ello, Urchin," the woman said affectionately, her voice thick and guttural as she spoke in Ilvan. "Your *madara* must be busy setting up for her holiday if you've come to pay me a visit at this time, child. How are you?"

Axe responded in kind. "*Madara* is very busy. But, not to worry, I've brought a friend with me today. Her name's Quinn. She's keepin' me company." Axe turned her eyes on Quinn expectantly, and Quinn flashed a tight smile by way of greeting at the mention of her name. The woman took a second glance, her eyes narrowing on the light purple strands of Quinn's hair.

"She's N'skari. You sure this is her sort of jig?"

"She comes from Norcasta. She's here with the dark prince," Axe said. Quinn ran her hand over her lips and jaw to cover the frown at the affectionate tone.

Does Axe feel something for Lazarus? she wondered. Not that it mattered. Axe was a child. Lazarus a man. There were bigger women to be concerned with, namely the urchin's *mother*.

"Ohhh," the bartender drawled. A mischievous twinkle lit her eyes. The woman turned to Quinn and switched to Norcastan, not knowing that Quinn had understood every word. "I'm Petra, Axe's aunt." Quinn's lips parted, a question on her tongue when Axe leaned forward.

"She's not my *real* aunt," Axe explained, "but Petra used to sail with *Madara*—she was with her when she found me. I have many aunts and uncles."

Quinn's brows furrowed but only said, "I see."

A shout rang out from the other side of the bar,

and Petra rolled her eyes. "I need to handle that. Is there anything I can get you two?"

"Two plum liquors and—"

"I'll have water," Quinn cut in. They both turned to her, squinting.

"Are you sure she's not prudish?" Petra asked, swapping back to Ilvan. "All those N'skari are over-modest and underfed, if you ask me."

Quinn frowned.

"Mostly," Axe replied in the same tongue before switching back. "You hungry?" she asked, turning her gaze back to Quinn.

"I could eat."

Axe smiled, and Quinn felt suspicion creeping in as Axe didn't hesitate to turn back to Petra and place an order. "Two house specials, then."

"Coming right up," Petra said while quickly turning on her heel, her similar smirk barely visible. She stormed across the bar toward two men who were busy trying to cave each other's face in with their fists. She grabbed both of them by their collars and wrenched them apart as one thought to take a cheap shot with a large stein, cracking it over the woman's head. Quinn watched intently, waiting for her to crumble.

The stein shattered first.

Petra shook off the shards and turned on the man who had attempted such a foolish endeavor. The man's eyes widened, and they continued to grow bigger as Petra dragged both of them through the bar. She clearly had more strength than her lean frame led others to believe as she kicked open the door and tossed them both into the streets without breaking a sweat.

"Try it again," she called after them, "and next time it'll be your hides I hang up on my walls." She took a moment and nodded to the various beasts she had pinned against the dark wood alongside the shop front windows.

Petra turned back to the bar, spirits running down her face and soaking her clothes as she snapped her fingers and pointed to the mess. A boy dressed in a ragged shirt and ill-fitting trousers jumped out from behind the counter and got to cleaning. Petra nodded once and went back to her work without another word.

"So," Quinn drawled. "Your aunt . . ."

"She's a skin shifter," Axe said in a bored voice.

Quinn reassessed the woman, but she knew from experience there wouldn't be any obvious signs of her magic. Skin shifters were a gray Maji with the only notable abilities of changing how hard their skin was. They could be tough as diamonds, making themselves nearly unbreakable— as she'd just seen. They also could make themselves as thin as the air itself, allowing them to travel through solid objects at will.

The latter was more problematic because it made them great thieves.

And assassins.

"She chooses to bartend?" Quinn asked, and Axe sighed.

"Aunt Petra was my *madara's* first mate. When *Madara* became Queen, she gave her the choice to be whatever she wanted. She chose this place and built it from the ground up with her own two hands," Axe said. They quieted as Petra came strolling over with two large mugs, one filled with purple liquid, the other clear.

Petra set them on the wooden table with a clank and said, "Your food will be right out."

Both Axe and Quinn muttered their thanks as she retreated to the bar.

"She had her choice of jobs, and she chose to own a tavern. That's interesting . . ." Quinn let her voice trail off as her mind began to turn the information over.

"Bein' the right-hand of a monarch ain't easy.

It's not a job you get to retire from." Axe gave her a slight smile and said, "But you probably knew that already."

"So, she chose to step down to lead a simple life instead of the wealth and riches of continuing to serve Imogen?" Quinn continued, ignoring her comment. She was well aware of the meaning behind Axe's inference. Being the right- or left-hand of a crown meant being tied to that crown until death. For most people.

Under a monarch, they're protected as part of their house, but when someone leaves with all the knowledge they've gained, they no longer have that protection . . . few are strong enough to survive the attempts on their life. Those that are able to fend off the foreign nations that came looking, afraid you'll spill their secrets, were usually powerful enough to go make their own kingdoms.

As was the way of the world.

You either had power or you didn't, and those with it rarely relinquished themselves to a life of novelty. Perhaps that was what interested her most about this Petra. She was a skin shifter, and yet, she chose to live in a hobble, despite what she could be.

Quinn didn't understand it.

"She chose simplicity over being hunted

anytime she was beyond these walls. Most of the country has forgotten my *madara* as the captain she was, and with her, Petra. The world outside has not. My aunt prefers this simple life next to the water," Axe said with more maturity than Quinn thought her capable of. The hinges of the moving panel in the bar made Quinn turn as Petra came out carrying two steaming dishes of rice with sausages and colorful peppers mixed in. On the bed of rice sat a massive lobster, cooked to perfection. Quinn's stomach rumbled.

"Enjoy your meal," she told them.

"Thanks, Aunty," Axe said around a mouthful of rice, falling back into her childish persona as she scarfed down several bites of food.

Quinn picked up her knife and fork and got to work cracking the lobster open. A rush of steam enveloped the air around her plate, and her mouth watered.

"How'd you become the Pirate Queen's daughter?" Quinn asked, before taking a bite. The succulent lobster meat melted on her tongue. Quinn held in a groan as she started shoveling lobster and rice into her as fast as her mouth could chew.

"I'll tell you," Axe said. "But first, I want to know more about how you ended up with Lord

Fierté." *Cheeky little sea urchin*, Quinn thought, shoveling more food in her mouth.

"I already told you that he saved me from being hanged," Quinn answered, plowing through the rest of her meal.

"Yes, but you also said your loyalty can't be bought," Axe countered, nibbling at the lobster tail on her plate. "If it can't be bought, then him saving you isn't why you are loyal to him, or his people." A sneaky little smile lit up her face when Quinn cleared her plate and then pointed her fork at Axe's.

"Loyalty is easy to understand, but how to earn it is more complicated—are you going to eat that?" Quinn asked, feeling more famished than she'd realized after so many days on the road.

Axe slid her plate over the table and took a long swig of her plum liquor as Quinn started to dig in. "We have all afternoon . . ." Axe said, letting her voice trail off.

Quinn licked the juices from her lips and sniffed at her mug. *It doesn't smell funny* . . . She took a tentative sip before gulping until half of it was gone.

"Ahh," Quinn said with a smile. She felt lighter than she had in a long while. That release of steam on the battlefield must've helped, and a full belly certainly didn't hurt. "Alright, I'll tell you since you gave me your lobster." She took another bite, and Axe watched, her expression a bit smug. "Lazarus saved me because he wanted a contract with me—"

"I knew it!" Axe exclaimed, slapping her hand on the table with a cackle.

Quinn frowned. "Knew what? That I'm his—"

"Hussy!"

Several eyes in the bar turned on them, but Quinn hardly noticed as she leveled the girl with a glare. "I am *not* his whore."

"But you just said—"

"I'm his vassal," Quinn interrupted, speaking over the child. "He wanted a contract with me because of what I am." At the expression on Axe's face, she added, "Not because of what's between my legs."

The girl frowned, taking another sip of her liquor. "I don't understand. Are you talkin' about the black magic stuff?"

"Yes," Quinn answered, then frowned. Never before had she talked this openly about her magic, but here she was discussing it with this girl. She narrowed her eyes on the red-haired urchin who appeared unperturbed as she swung her legs back and forth under the table, accidentally hitting Quinn's shin.

"Oops," she said with a cringe.

"It's fine," Quinn said, her suspicion lowering. "Lazarus saved me from the gallows because he wanted my magic. The more I traveled with him . . . things changed." She let the sentence drop, her mind starting down the twisted path of the past few weeks when Axe pulled her out of it.

"What do you mean?"

"Well," Quinn said, pushing aside Axe's half-eaten plate. She was so full; she couldn't touch another bite. "Lazarus proved to me he didn't want me as a slave, even though what he really wants me for has become complicated . . ." Again, Quinn stopped herself and frowned. This sort of easygoing conversation wasn't like her. Something was off. The more she thought about it, the more the fullness of her stomach and the scent of smoke drifted her into a relaxed state.

Quinn grimaced. She had a feeling what was causing it and that she'd miscalculated the effects of the pipe smoke and what it might have on her system.

"So, Lazarus likes you?" Axe pressed.

"I don't know," Quinn answered. "I'm not sure 'like' is the word I would use for whatever we are." She ran a hand through her hair and sighed softly.

"Lazarus understands me. He doesn't judge me for the things I've done or still do. He's controlling and manipulative and sometimes cruel, but—" She stopped herself, slapping a hand over her mouth. She was about to tell Axe that those were the things she liked about him, but that was crossing a line— no matter the reason she said it. Those who ran their mouth under the influence of herbs or drink were still liable for the consequences of their actions, and she was no different.

"I've got to be honest with you," Axe said, draining the rest of her liquor. "I get what you see in him, but I've no idea what he sees in you." Quinn blinked, then frowned. "I mean, look at him, doin' his whole rugged man thing, and then look at you"—she motioned to Quinn distastefully—"you look like a drowned rat. It's like you're not even tryin'—"

"Because I'm not," Quinn replied stiffly.

"Exactly," Axe said, gesticulating wildly. "You're better than the other N'skari I've met, but that's not sayin' much. Lord Fierté needs a woman with a little more *spice*." She wiggled her eyebrows suggestively, and Quinn stared, completely dumbfounded about how the conversation had taken this turn. "You're more suited to one of these blokes." She waved at the table a few feet over, and their heads turned. Quinn got a sinking feeling in her gut when two of the men leaned toward them, grinning through chapped lips with their yellowed teeth.

"Yer a pretty lass," one of them said in thickly accented Norcastan.

"See? They'd make *so* much more sense," Axe started. "You boys should try your hand. She's a hussy, so it's not like she's hard to impress——"

"For the last time, I'm not a whore," Quinn snapped in annoyance. The men threw their heads back and laughed jovially.

"We doona judge, Beauty," another one said. His viridian eyes were locked on the neckline of her thick burlap shirt as it hung low. Quinn narrowed her eyes as the four of them got to their feet and came to stand around the small table.

The breath in Quinn's throat constricted as they brushed too close. "The Queen's holiday be starting soon, and we need a young lass to enjoy for the week——"

"No," Quinn said coolly, her eyes going cold. Three of the four men instantly backed off, but the one who was talking didn't like that answer.

"If the Queen's bairn be right with it . . ." He leaned in, and his breath smelled of spirits, making her meal curdle in her stomach. Quinn gripped the edge of the table as a hand closed over her thigh and lips brushed the nape of her neck.

"I wouldn't do that," Axe said in a sing-song voice with a sigh. "I thought she'd be interested, but apparently not. You might want to back off before she—"

Quinn's arm reached between his legs, her fingers curling around his jewels, gripping him with an unyielding force. The man grunted, his jaw clenching in discomfort.

"Come now, I didn't mean—" His words cut off with a squeak as Quinn squeezed tighter, getting to her feet. She backed the man up until his legs hit the table he'd been sitting at.

"I'll be damned," Axe said. "You *do* have some spice. I take it back. I might be alright with you takin' him." Quinn wasn't in the mood for her antics anymore. Axe had pushed just a hair too far, as had the man who now trembled before her.

"One twist of my wrist and you won't be having any fun during the holiday," Quinn said through gritted teeth. "Two twists and I might just break your favorite part." She smiled wickedly as her veins turned black. The gathering audience of patrons moved away as Petra came around the bar.

"What's the meaning of this?" she asked, but Quinn ignored her.

"If you ever so much as touch me again, I'll cut your hands off and make you eat them. Understood?"

The man's nodded response and downcast eyes cooled the edge of her temper. She dropped her hand, turning to leave and finding Axe already gone.

She clenched her teeth hard and cursed under her breath as she twisted around to storm out the front door, and instead found her path blocked.

Lazarus had arrived, and judging by his expression, he wasn't pleased.

Shackles of Control

"She was beautiful chaos; as uncontrollable as a storm."
— *Lazarus Fierté, soul eater, heir to Norcasta, territorial prince*

He'd tracked her to a bar called the *Opal Room*, but nothing prepared him for the surge of fire that licked through his veins when he found her sitting with a man at her side, leaning in close. *Too close.* His own hands curled inwards, forming fists as the brute pawed at her beneath the table. Lips touched her skin and the souls inside him called for blood.

Violence tinged the air as Quinn froze.

Over her head, he caught the expression on Axe's face as she watched the whole thing play out. *Blatant guilt.*

He stepped into the bar, and Quinn exploded. Moving faster than he could track, she stood up with her hand anchored between the man's legs as she shoved him back against another table. There was a quiet exchange of words that ended with him wide-eyed. Lazarus tensed, not liking that she was pushed, nor that she was touching him—whatever the reason.

He knew he shouldn't feel that. He should let his vassal handle this, as she was more than capable. Yet . . . he couldn't stop himself from crossing the threshold, inhaling the sweet scents of smoke. Axe looked up at that moment, and her lips parted before she bolted from her chair and out the back. Quinn didn't even glance in her direction until she'd finished making her threat to the man. He could feel her anger seething as she turned to leave and came face-to-face with him.

"Get out of my way," she breathed. A thin sheen of sweat coated her skin, and her eyes were clouded over. Lazarus frowned.

"We need to talk," he said. Her pale cheeks had turned a shade of pink and were steadily darkening.

It took great amounts of exercise to make Quinn break a sweat . . . he blinked, and his eyes slid to the pipe on the table beside him.

"I don't drink spirits." That's what she'd said. The only time he'd seen her like this was after the alcohol she'd accidentally consumed flowed through her. Given the amount of smoke in the establishment and her low tolerance, he was fairly certain what was going on here, and that he needed to get her back to the palace. Now.

"I don't want to talk to you," Quinn growled, stomping past him. She slammed her shoulder into his, and he grimaced.

Stupid, stupid girl.

"Quinn, you're not in your right mind—"

Metal hinges screeched and a thud reverberated as the door hit the wooden frame.

Lazarus turned, but Quinn was already gone.

He ran a hand over his jaw and up his face, snagging his hair as he let out a heavy sigh. Quinn was going to get herself killed or lose him this alliance if she kept at it.

He shook his head and left the bar. In the open air, her scent was blended among many. He had to follow her blackened footprints and the taint of her magic as she weaved through the crowds. After several minutes and a few wrong turns that she corrected, he saw a lavender head duck behind the palace gate. Her crystalline eyes, unfocused and bloodshot, swept over the plaza behind her, searching for anyone that dared to follow. He suspected it was only her inebriation that stopped her from seeing him as he pushed through the throng of people and into the courtyard. He tracked her back to her room, where the door was just swinging shut. He slipped his foot in the threshold, stopping it from closing.

Quinn stood with her back to him, hands fisted in her hair as she let out a sound somewhere between a growl and groan, cursing spirits and all things mind-altering under her breath. She stilled, her hands falling to her sides as she slowly turned and leveled him with cold blue eyes.

Lazarus' breath caught in his throat as he stepped through the door and let it fall closed behind him. The lock clicked shut.

"You followed me," she said, eyes flashing. "I told you I don't want to talk."

"You also told me you wouldn't be a hindrance, and then an hour later, I find you holding a man by his balls," Lazarus replied stiffly. Heat coursed through his veins as something in his chest tightened.

"He put his hands where they didn't belong," Quinn answered, crossing her arms over her chest. She shifted side to side as if she were uneasy. He could sense the restlessness inside her.

You and me both, saevyana. He cursed himself as soon as the thought came to him.

He shouldn't be thinking of her as that, let alone giving a name to it.

Yet, he couldn't help himself.

"That he did," he said, staring at the place along her neck that the fool had thought to kiss. Lazarus was considering paying him a visit when he was done here. "But it doesn't excuse that you left when I was trying to speak with you—for this exact reason. Your magic has grown, and you aren't always in complete control of it. We need to talk about—"

"You want to talk about something?" she interrupted, a glint of malice in her expression. A dark glee that glittered in her gaze as she moved closer. "Sure, let's talk." Quinn's svelte frame shifted as she stared up at him. "Let's talk about that kiss."

Lazarus pressed his lips together so she didn't

see the way his tongue traced his teeth at the mention of it. "This isn't the time," he replied.

She smiled, and it was wicked. Mazzulah was dancing in her eyes this day, and he knew there would be no reasoning. Not when she was like this.

"Not the time?" she asked softly. "Pray tell—when *is* the time? When I'm not here? When you're telling the others how you'll handle me? When you're reasoning with yourself that your reactions are normal and that I'm simply a vassal and nothing more?" She came closer, lithe and silent despite her altered state of mind. Her hand came up to touch the fabric on his tunic. She trailed them over his chest as she moved to circle him.

"Quinn, you do not want to push me—"

"Don't I?" The air thickened with tension and magic.

Deadly.

Potent.

Delicious.

He inhaled deeply, and a hint of madness touched him as the souls beneath his skin coiled and writhed. *For her.* They craved chaos, and she was as close to it as they could get.

He was a masochist. It had been a mistake; coming here, trying to reason with this woman.

But then, he was always drawn to the monsters of the world.

Quinn was no different.

"Tell me, Lazarus," she whispered in his ear as she circled behind him. Her breath fanned his skin as one of her arms skated around his side and her palm came to rest against his chest. "Do you toy with me because you can't help it? Or is this just another game we play?"

He swallowed as the hand on his chest turned ashen, the veins under her skin darkening. *In Mazzulah's grip, indeed.*

Anxiety stirred within him, clawing its way out of his flesh to greet its master.

He wondered if she realized she was doing it, or if this was just another slip.

His heart pounded at the idea of having to coax her from the edge of mania, because only one method would.

His hand came up as he locked his fingers with hers. Lazarus felt the woman at his back still against him. Her cool breath invaded his senses as her body pressed tightly against his, the feel of her breasts pushed against him bringing dangerous thoughts to mind. Lazarus turned sharply, yanking her hand down and pulling her flush against his chest. Her breaths grew shallow, her pupils expanding as she inhaled his scent. The raw expression on her face made him weak.

"Play? As you are right now? Cajoling my own fears to come to the surface so that you can control me as you do others?" He leaned in close, his lips skated the line of her jaw as he whispered in her ear. "Are you sure it's me playing games, Quinn?" His warm breath drifted over her skin. "Or is it you?" She shuddered.

Quinn clenched her hand, and the anxiety spun out of control.

Lazarus drew back as she raised her other hand between them and black wisps shot from beneath the rich blue of his tunic, drawn out from his chest. They curled into her palm, forming an orb before fracturing apart.

Her fingers slipped from his as his body was thrown. His back hit the wall but did not drop as those tendrils of fear formed manacles around his wrists and ankles.

She'd pulled on his emotions and turned his fear into a tangible weapon with little more than a thought. He knew he should be afraid. He knew he should put her down like he would a rabid animal

—before she learned the power she held. Before she learned what she was truly capable of.

And though it may have crossed his mind briefly, as she came to stand before him—brilliant in her savagery—he shoved them away.

No. He could not. He *would* not. The voices begged for her touch, and he found himself enthralled as she leaned in. Her lips were only a hairsbreadth from his as she whispered, "Why did you kiss me, Lazarus?"

His lips parted on their own accord as he stared down at her. The vicious little creature he couldn't leave be. The one woman in this world that could best him—and the one woman that he couldn't deny himself. He took her from a prison cell and made her his—even if only in contract.

But now he wanted more. He wanted *everything*.

That was a dangerous thought for a would-be king to have.

The only thing he wouldn't give up to have her was his crown.

And the crown was the very reason he had sought her out to begin with.

Oh, how Fortuna loved to play. The gods had to have a wayward sense of humor to put her in his path. To make him crave her like this; crave to use her, crave to *take* her—as a man took a woman.

Her lips brushed his when she didn't get her answer. *So soft, so supple . . .* her teeth nipped at his bottom lip and heat doused his veins as he felt himself grow and thicken. He arched forward to bite her back when she danced to the side, a mischievous grin on her face.

"You can end this, Lazarus," she said in a sultry voice. Quinn rested a pale hand on his chest and let it slowly trail downward. "Tell me why you kissed me. Tell me if you're trying to—" Her voice broke off as her fingers traced his length through his trousers, and a hiss escaped through his clenched teeth.

He'd called her stupid when she was brash, but the truth was that Quinn wasn't stupid. She was cruel; she was wicked. She was everything she needed to be. Everything the world had made her to be and everything he would strengthen if only for his own purposes.

Lazarus pulled against the manacles, lust and violence colliding within him in a frenzy.

She played a dangerous game, and judging by the smirk she wore—Quinn knew it.

"I kissed you to pull you back," he bit out—

both wanting to stop this torment and not wanting it to end. It made no sense, but neither did he when it came to her.

She stepped closer again, letting her fingers run up and down his length in slow, tantalizing motions. Quinn leaned forward, letting her lips brush over the skin of his neck as she whispered, "Why did you want to pull me back?"

"You know why—" He started to answer but cut himself off with a muttered grunt as she bit down on his earlobe. Her sharp little teeth pierced his skin right before she sucked the sting away with her tongue and lips. He let out a groan as his vision started to darken.

"Tell me—"

Quinn didn't get to her demand. The shackles broke as the souls within rose up and with them, Lazarus' fury . . . and his hunger.

The black tendrils shattered as if they had been made of solid material and not the combination of his fear and hers. With their destruction, however, her power to control him snapped as well. Lazarus pivoted swiftly, slamming Quinn to the wall by her hips.

She let out a gasp as he grabbed her by the back of her thighs and lifted her from the ground, spreading her legs to wrap around him as he ground himself against her. A moan slipped from between her lips.

The fervor worsened as he growled, "Do you understand now, Quinn?" Using his hips to pin her, he raised both her arms over her head, leashing her wrists with one hand. The other came back down to grab a handful of her backside, boosting her and letting her feel the full force of his arousal. Quinn stilled.

"You crave control as much as you crave me." Her voice was husky with desire as she arched into him. "Oh, but you wish you didn't." She laughed, and it was the sound of that hoarse chuckle that was his undoing.

His nails bit into the plumpness of her rear through her leather pants, and when Quinn's lips parted once more, he slanted forward, pressing his mouth to hers. His tongue sought all that she offered, and Quinn groaned, kissing him back with an intensity that no woman he'd ever touched could even come close to. Lazarus worked her into a frenzy, pressing against the damp place between her thighs as he coaxed her mouth into submission.

Just when his control started to slip, and he

worried he wouldn't be able to stop, Lazarus stepped away and dropped her.

Quinn's feet hit the ground with a thud and she stumbled, gaping up at him for a moment in disbelief before her expression transformed into one of scowling irritation.

"You are my vassal, and I'm your lord—soon to be king. I took you because you're a fear twister, and even if I want you in other ways, it's a line I will not cross again. Do not test me on this, Quinn, or you'll regret it." Lazarus turned and strode for the door, biting the inside of his cheek as he left her there— hoping she couldn't see through his lie as easily as he could.

If Quinn pushed him again, he wasn't sure he'd be able to walk away.

Marked by the Gods

"The gods are fickle creatures, but then, so are men."
— *Draeven Adelmar, vassal of House Fierté, rage thief*

Draeven felt the pit of exhaustion expand in his mind, a foggy cloud hanging over his thoughts. Try as he might to keep pushing through it, he knew that he was nearing a blackout. The rage had dissipated enough so that he wasn't at risk of losing control, but in its wake came the fatigue from a battle hard-won. While the rest of his comrades had strode into the Pirate Queen's palace with their heads and minds clear and present,

Draeven had waged a silent war with himself every step of the way.

Even now, hours after he'd been released from Lazarus' chambers to perform some discrete reconnaissance on the Queen's advisor, he found himself wavering on his feet, focusing far too much on the thoughts inside his head rather than his surroundings. He had followed Zorel throughout the castle for the last several hours, watching the man talk with various people. Draeven couldn't place the advisor's face from anywhere in particular. On the outside, he appeared like any other court official, and as much as Draeven wished that were true, he feared that his instincts were not wrong.

Draeven was so wrapped up in his own musings that he didn't hear the hard, repetitive tapping of footsteps against the stone floor until he was nearly upon his chamber door. He paused, confusion and surprise echoing across his features as he noticed the woman leaning against the archway—a glower on her face.

"You're late," Quinn snapped. "I thought you would be here by now. Not skulking around."

Draeven blinked at her in confusion. "I was not skulking around," he said absently as he bypassed the woman to unlatch his chamber door. Leaving it to swing open on its own, he gestured—as any gentleman would—for her to go first. Quinn narrowed her eyes and shook her head. Draeven sighed and stepped through into the room, glancing around before nodding at her that they were alone. "What's this about? Why are you here?"

When Quinn didn't immediately respond, Draeven eyed her with increasing frustration. His brows furrowed together as he tried to shove the emotion away. "If you've come to talk about Lazarus' words earlier—" he started, uncertain and simply far too tired to deal with an angry fear twister at the present. Quinn was someone he would much rather leave for Lazarus to deal with, and not himself. He simply didn't know what to do with her.

"That's not what this is about," she interrupted him, her lips curving down further. Truth be told, if the woman ever did smile, Draeven feared what it would mean. Shaking his head, he closed the door before continuing into the room, glancing her way as he rounded one of the chamber lounges and sank onto the cushion with a sigh. "I came about something else."

"Well, then," he gestured for her to continue. "I'm happy to help." Quinn narrowed her eyes at his half-hearted, sardonic tone. "What can I do for you?" Ignoring her, he leaned forward, steepling his fingers with his elbows propped on his knees. "What would bring you to my chambers so late?" he asked, letting the attitude drop. The buzzing in his temples made much of the room hazy despite the candles scattered about. He sighed heavily, tired of bickering, tired of being angry, tired of feeling much anything at all.

"I need to show you something," she said.

His brows lifted lazily. "What is it?" he asked with a frown.

Quinn paced across the room, turning on her heel and then pacing back. "It's . . . a mark," she finally said. "It wasn't there before, but after what happened in the mountains . . ." Quinn paused, and a struggle stretched over her expression before a veil of determination set in. "It doesn't seem to be going away."

"A mark? Is it an old wound?" Draeven stood up and moved forward, the fog of his mind clearing briefly to make way for concern. Quinn, on the other hand, froze at his sharp movement and glared at him, making him pause and drop his arms. "I can't very well take a look at your wound if you won't let me touch you," he said tersely.

"It's not a wound," she replied.

"Then what is it? You said a mark. If not a wound, then . . ." he trailed off, waiting for her to explain.

"It wasn't there before," Quinn stated. "I thought I felt something after Lazarus and I returned from the mountains. A strange soreness in my side, but the mark didn't appear until after the battle."

"Where is it?" he asked.

Quinn dropped her arms, still hesitant. Draeven didn't push her. She would either show him or she wouldn't, and him pushing her wasn't going to change her decision either way.

He felt his shoulders droop as he exhaled another heavy breath. The fatigue that followed was almost as difficult to handle as the rage when he consumed it. Usually, it was gone by now, but Quinn's had been terrible. He'd never felt a madness quite like he did in those hours, and the exhaustion that followed was equally troubling. Draeven considered turning away, his eyes fell on the bed across the room.

Quinn stepped in front of him, drawing his

attention again. She reached down, grasping at the edges of her shirt and lifting it. Even in the dim light, he could make out a black rounded mark—the imprint of a snake swallowing its own tail—visible just above her leathers.

He lifted a hand, pointedly ignoring how the limb trembled, though it wasn't in fear. His warm fingers found the line of her trousers and drew the tight material down so that it was completely revealed. The marking was no more than the length of his pinky, almost a perfect circle.

"You can drop your shirt now," he said with a sigh.

Quinn asked, "Do you know what it is? Is it dangerous?"

He shook his head. "It's not dangerous," he assured her, striding past as he went to the bed. He bent over to remove his boots, letting the first one drop on the floor and then the other before he snatched them both up and laid them side by side against the end post. "It's a mark of your ascension. Every Maji gets one. Nothing to be concerned with at all."

"So, it's normal, then?" She sounded unsure.

"As normal as Maji can be," Draeven replied

drily. "I have one, myself. They can be in various places. It all depends. It's a symbol of having made it through to the other side. Of being chosen by the gods."

Draeven didn't say it aloud, but in his thoughts, the reminder of what his parents had told him—of how honored all Maji should be to be chosen by the very gods that created this world—it grated on his already strained nerves. Not all Maji were as fortunate to be gifted with light abilities as his parents had been. Some—like him—were only chosen to be the bearers of the world's wrath. *A regrettable position*, he thought to himself.

"Draeven." From the sharpness in her voice, it was clear that Quinn had been trying to gain his attention for some time.

He shook his head as if he could shake away all of his unpleasant thoughts and lifted his head to meet her eyes from across the room. "Yes? Sorry. What did you say?"

Quinn eyed him but spoke again. "You said that you have a marking as well."

Draeven scrubbed a hand down his face, resting that hand on his jaw as he got to the end and using it to crack his neck. "Of course," he said. "Like I said before, all Maji get one. It happens with the ascension."

"Can I see yours?" she asked abruptly.

Draeven paused. "You . . . want to see my mark?" he asked, sure he had heard her wrong.

"Yes. I want to see if it's any different than mine."

Draeven stood up, his lips thinning out as he strode back across the room. He did not mind touch so much as she seemed to, but knowing her aversion to physical contact made him wary as he approached her. "To my knowledge, there has never been the same mark on two different Maji," he said, stopping before her. Clear blue eyes stared back at him, and despite the frenzy of rage he had stolen from her before, he could sense that there was still more beneath the surface. He hid the shudder that ran through him well.

"I still want to see," she said.

Draeven turned and stripped off his shirt, tossing it toward the end of the bed. The tips of her fingers caressed the skin of his left shoulder blade where his mark was. He stiffened at the coldness of her touch, like stone floors in the winter. The sensation was jarring.

"It looks like an inferno," she commented. "Why is that?"

"I don't know," he replied honestly. "I suppose the gods might have something to do with it, or perhaps the power chooses the image. Fire is often associated with rage. I always assumed that was the connection."

"I have a snake," Quinn pointed out.

Turning and glancing over his shoulder, he watched as her brow puckered while she traced the edges of the ring of fire that was burned into not just his flesh, but his very soul.

"From what I've been told, your ascension wasn't exactly under normal circumstances," Draeven said. "But aside from what happened in the spring—"

Quinn quickly dropped her hand. "What do you know?"

Sensing her growing ire, Draeven stepped away, reaching for his shirt again and quickly tugging it on once more. "All I know is what Lazarus has told me." He straightened his shoulders; certain he could still feel the ghost of her frozen hands on his back.

"What has he told you?" she demanded.

"Enough," he replied vaguely, earning another furious scowl from her. "Aside from what happened, however, I would assume that you have the imprint of a snake because of the god of fear. It's been said he was the father of dragons and their ancestors—snakes."

She harrumphed, but the answer seemed to satisfy her. "How'd you get yours?" she demanded.

Draeven stiffened, his muscles bunching beneath his newly redonned shirt as he turned away from her. His mouth went dry. Echoes of horrified screams assaulted him. Visions of a fire burning so hot that it scalded him from the inside out. The wave of his rage as it swallowed him whole, a gigantic beast chomping down on his bones until there was nothing left inside of him but the pounding and the bloodlust.

Through gritted teeth, Draeven answered, "I got mine as you got yours. After my ascension." It was all he could do to keep his voice as even as possible. Unaltered by the images in his head. Light. Easy. Welcoming. He never again wanted to feel the wrath of his own anger as it consumed him. For as long as he lived, he couldn't ever take back what he might have done—or what he might yet still do—in the midst of such rage.

Draeven shook his head, attempting to ward off

the unwanted memories. He shoved them back, only to realize Quinn had been speaking to him the entire time.

"—like mine."

Draeven's lips parted, and he looked at her with a grimace. "What's like yours?" he asked.

"I said, your mark is in a circle. Like mine. Are all of them like that?"

Draeven frowned and gestured for her to step forward as a dull resonating drum began to beat inside his head. The end of his exhaustion drawing near. He needed to get Quinn out of his chambers or leave to find somewhere to bed down for the night, sooner rather than later, or he risked crashing right where he stood. "Let me see yours again."

Turning her side back to him, Quinn reached down and lifted her shirt once more without preamble, shuffling down her trousers for him to peer at the blackened mark upon her skin. Draeven traced the edge of his fingertip around the outside of the snake. *Yes*, he thought, *a perfect circle. . .*

"It's—" he began, only to stop as a knock sounded on his door, and without a pause, the noise of the handle unlatching sounded throughout the room. Draeven knew who it was before the man spoke; only one person had the sanction to intrude on his chambers without waiting for an answer.

"Draeven, I've come to—" Lazarus' voice came to an abrupt halt as Draeven stood up and Quinn dropped her shirt. The dull thud in his skull grew increasingly painful. One look at his expression told Draeven that he had already noticed Quinn's exposed skin—and his own hand caressing it—and Lazarus was not happy.

With a sigh, he moved away from her. "I think it's time I retired for the evening," Draeven said with a wince. He reached the edge of the bed and grabbed his boots, leaning over to quickly tug them back on.

"This is your room," Quinn pointed out.

Draeven glanced between her to Lazarus before shaking his head. "I think I'll sleep in Dominicus' room tonight."

"What if he's not there?" Quinn pointed out.

Draeven huffed out a breath as he reached the door and called over his shoulder, "Then in the stables. It wouldn't be the first time." With that, he strode out into the hallway and closed the door behind him, leaving the two of them to stew and linger without him.

As misfortune would have it, Dominicus was not

in his room, as Quinn had suggested. His knock went unanswered, which only served to double his weariness as he marched out of the Queen's palace toward the stables. Upon reaching them, he stopped just inside and inhaled the scent of sweat and hay. A quick gander around told him that the place was empty except for the beasts in their stalls.

Heading down the line, Draeven's feet shuffled until he found an empty stall. It appeared someone had taken their horse out for duty and the stable hands had cleaned the quarters and tossed in clean hay. As soon as he had the stall door closed, Draeven fell face first into the pile of fresh straw.

The ache against his temples ballooned into impossible proportions. No living, breathing man should take the amount of pain he had. The gods marked him with the ring of fire, a rage all-consuming and everlasting. It was a powerful gift bestowed upon him, but with power . . . there came consequences.

As Draeven lay there, surrounded by the wafting smells of dirt and horse feed, gritting his teeth against the bottomless pit of his lethargy and pain—he wished for the impossible. He wished for all of the rage to disappear. He wished to give back this horrendous gift. He wished the mark of the gods would disappear. And even as oblivion reached out its sickeningly long fingers, gripping him by the throat and limbs to drag him into the waiting void, he wished for one last thing.

Peace.

Like Calls to Like

"Some men live for honor, others for love, and even still there
are those that live for something so few survive. Chaos."
— Lazarus Fierté, soul eater, heir to Norcasta, indomitable
prince

The door clicked shut behind him, but Lazarus didn't move. He peered at her through the dimly lit room, noting how the muscles in her shoulders locked. Her head was bowed at an angle, but not in reverence. Her face was tilted slightly down, her cold blue eyes staring at nothing in particular. The angle of her jaw and cheekbone was striking, sharp enough to cut. The vein in her neck pulsed.

His eyes traveled down the slender column of her throat to the rumpled shirt she wore. The edge folded at an awkward place, just over her left hip, revealing an inch of pale skin. Dark blotches broke it up, but there wasn't enough visible for him to tell what the mark actually was beyond a faint guess.

Quinn cleared her throat and straightened out, folding her arms over her chest. It would have amused him, had he not just found her with her shirt up and his left-hand looking on while tracing her skin with his fingers.

The only saving grace for Draeven was that Lazarus knew he wouldn't touch Quinn in that way. If not because she was *his*, but because the man had softer tastes than Lazarus. He preferred them pretty and soft spoken. Draeven liked his women as damsels, sweet and pliable. Gentle.

Quinn might be beautiful, but when she spoke with a softness, it wasn't out of shyness or reserve. When Quinn spoke softly, all around her would do better to be wary and fear what her words meant. Draeven knew that. Lazarus knew that he knew that —but Quinn didn't.

"What do you want?" she asked him.

He motioned to the room before her with one hand. "I came to see my left-hand, but it seems you scared him off." She scowled, her violet brows drawing together as a pucker formed between them.

"*I* scared him off?" she asked, letting out a huff. "He was helping me before you walked in. So, what did you want? What was so urgent that you had to come meet with him in the middle of the night?" She narrowed her eyes, and the corner of Lazarus' lips turned upward.

"I could ask you the same, and unlike me, you would have to answer."

She scoffed, and the grin slipped from his lips.

He might like the hard edge around her and the cold touch of her skin, but the way she mocked him was exactly why he could not have her as he wanted.

His crown would not withstand it.

"Answer?" she asked. Her arms dropped to her sides, and she took a step forward, a derisive smile forming on her lips. "You think that with enough time and careful manipulations I'll be just like the others, don't you? That you can ask anything of me, and I'll offer it up without thought to ask for the same in return?"

He stared down at her, not sure if provoking her was wise. He needed to maintain control, but the closer she came, the more it slipped away as the beasts beneath his skin stirred. Her presence rattled them as nothing else did, and while he needed to restrain them, he wasn't sure he wanted it to stop either. Something about her kept him rooted to the floor when he should have turned and left her to her antics.

Quinn stepped forward, coming so close they were only inches from touching.

Lazarus took a harsh breath and spoke.

"If you think that I can ask anything of them and they give it without thought, you don't see as much as you think you do."

"I see enough," she answered.

"You see what you want to see," he replied. She turned to walk away, and he grabbed her wrist, not pulling but preventing her from moving all the same. Quinn paused, but she didn't look at him. She stood there, as if she were waiting for something.

"You wanted Draeven and he's gone now. You're still here. So, what do you want?" she asked eventually.

Lazarus had many ways he could answer her,

from demanding what she was doing here, to letting her go—as he probably should. All his life he'd been a man that put his ambitions first. He acted in the better interest of himself, and then later, his house. Quinn was part of his house, but she was right about one thing.

She'd never be like the rest of them.

It wasn't her power alone that made it so, but something inside her that, like him, couldn't help but crave the chaos.

Some people thought it a pit of despair.

For some, it was.

But for an even smaller number of persons, chaos was life. There was order in the disorder. A method to the madness. In the confusion, some found themselves and even fewer found something far more precious.

Purpose.

In this, he and Quinn were more alike than any other souls in all of the Sirian continent.

So many had lost themselves, lost their families, lost their values, lost everything to the chaos.

But not in their case. Something in it resonated within them.

Like calls to like.

And that was why he was still here instead of

leaving as he knew he should. There was a thrill in playing these games with her, and even if he couldn't have what he wanted, he wondered if he'd ever truly be able to give this up.

"What do you want?" she repeated again. Many things came to mind, but he pushed them all aside.

"It's been a week," he said.

She turned, raising a brow. "You want an answer but you've yet to ask a question."

"Your stomach"—he released her wrist to let his finger trail down her side and grasp the edge of her shirt—"there's a mark on it, but I had all slave brands removed. Where and how did you get it?"

She blinked, but he hadn't pulled at the fabric, instead waiting to see what she'd say, how she'd respond.

He was not disappointed.

She stepped back, and the material slipped from his fingers. Quinn grabbed a handful of her shirt and pulled it up, then pinched the band of her trousers and tugged them down. There, burned in her skin below her navel and to the left, was a mark.

"It's my mark of ascension. It showed up after the battle outside of Tritol. Draeven told me all Maji have one," she said. He leaned forward, unaware he was extending his hand until she stepped to the side. Lazarus paused, swallowing hard.

"They do. Yours is quite interesting . . ." He trailed off. She lifted a brow but did not ask what he meant. Lazarus knew why. She had something else she would ask of him.

In this case, he wasn't sure if he should be relieved or not.

Maji had a mark that represented their magic, but it was also specific to them. Hers was the ouroboros. They were seen as a sign of life and death. A mark of rebirth.

He wondered why the gods would place such a mark upon her.

"I have a snake beneath my skin. I don't find it all that strange the gods might put another on me. Neiss was the god of fear, and he was said to have snakes for hair that struck fear even into the hearts of the other gods." He nodded.

"Perhaps," he answered. *Or perhaps the gods meddled more than men believed.* Something about the mark unsettled him. He pushed that thought aside as she dropped her shirt.

"I want to see your mark," she replied.

He wasn't shocked by the request. If she'd come to Draeven about her own mark, as he suspected she had, then she'd be curious about the marks of others—how the gods chose to claim them.

He reached for his tunic, and her eyes tracked the motion. Heat settled in his veins as the souls took notice. Lazarus pulled at the fabric, sliding it up his chest until he held it almost to his neck. Quinn squinted, stepping forward once again.

"You have so many—"

"Here," he pointed over his heart. She tilted her head, moving closer. He ignored the scent of her as it drifted over him.

"I don't understand . . ." Her lips parted, and she tilted her head. "They're attacking it."

He didn't say anything as she lifted a hand, her fingers brushing over the center of his sternum. The beasts paused, turning their attention toward her as she traced the outline.

The sensation of her cool fingers over his heated skin made him catch his breath, only to inhale the delectable aroma of her magic. His muscles strained, wanting to reach for the woman that tortured him.

After a long pause, she looked up at him.

"Why do they attack yours?"

"I let you see. I don't have to answer," he replied, starting to pull away. She reached up with her other hand and wrapped it around his bicep, digging her nails in like claws.

"Actually, I never asked. Therefore, you never answered." She smiled faintly as her words came back to him.

I want to see your mark.

Not a question, but an implied request. He narrowed his eyes at her, not truly angry, but frustrated that he seemed to be losing this battle of wills with her.

"A Maji's mark is tied to their soul, as is their magic. When you were drained of your magic and the basilisk with you, the result was that you merged. The creature is now part of you and you it." She frowned.

"I don't see what that has to do with the creatures beneath your skin attacking your mark," she whispered.

He leaned forward until their lips were only a hairsbreadth apart.

"I consumed them. They only exist because my magic keeps them alive. In turn, they each eat away at pieces of my own soul." He sensed the shiver that ran through her. Whatever magic inside of Neiss that bound them together also bound her to him as a result.

"If that's true, one day you'll have no soul at all," she said.

He swallowed against the dryness in his throat. Lazarus was not a man that feared easily. He was not intimidated by gods he could not see. He bowed to no one in this life, but he strongly suspected what the price of that might be.

"Perhaps." He stepped away, and her hands fell to her sides once more. Lazarus lowered his shirt, covering the only proof of who and what he was. "But what use does a man have for a soul if his enemies can't kill him?"

Lazarus turned to leave when her voice stopped him.

"They might not be able to, but there is one thing that none of us can outrun no matter how powerful we might be." She paused, letting the quiet settle between them. Lazarus felt the silence creep up the ridges of his spine and delve beneath his skin to swim with the souls he'd consumed. "Do you know what that is?" she finally asked him.

"Time?" He guessed the answer, looking over his shoulder as he did.

"No. While I don't know it, I imagine there are ways to outrun even that. The thing that no one ever escapes is fear." Her eyes glowed brighter for a moment. The depth of the blue deeper and vaster than any ocean, and even more treacherous. "And that's because fear lives within its victims always. From the moment they are born, to the moment they perish under the watchful eyes of the gods. It can make a prideful man beg for death. It can make a strong man break. And it does all of this without laying a finger on them. Fear can eat you alive, from the inside out, until you would do anything for the escape of the dark realm."

"I don't fear death," he said.

"No," she agreed, nodding her head. "You fear losing control of yourself, and it makes me wonder why. For someone that doesn't value their soul, you don't want to lose it."

Lazarus didn't respond as he let himself out. Yet, still, the echo of her words rang in his ears. Quinn had no idea how right she was.

Battle for Ilvas

"In a land of sheep, it pays to be a wolf."
— *Quinn Darkova, vassal of House Fierté, fear twister*

Quinn's hand clenched around the iron railing overlooking the Bay of Tritol. Across the surface of the glimmering water, two ships faced off. To one side, a black flag with a skeleton queen floated on the slight breeze as the heat of Leviticus' eye bore down on the quickly gathering crowd. On the other side, a white flag bearing two crossed axes waved over a red-haired girl.

Axe's lips were drawn in a smirk as she stared

over the strip of water at the opposing vessel her mother commanded. Imogen's long slender fingers wrapped around the wooden notches of the wheel, turning it slightly. A wind whipped through the bay, blowing the dark strands of her hair from her face. There was a mischievous twinkle in her eyes, something reminiscent of the stories of the pirate she had once been before she became Queen.

"Two of a kind, aren't they?" a voice said, drawing Quinn away from her observations.

Zorel, Imogen's advisor, joined her against the railing as the battle began with the firing of cannons in the distance. The shock of the noise startled some of the crowd but was quickly met with a deafening roar as the two ships began moving.

"They do know how to put on a show," Quinn agreed, returning her gaze back to the scene before her where the winds and waters had the two vessels gaining speed against one another as they cut through the choppy surface.

"They look forward to this every year," Zorel admitted. "It is the one week that my Queen gets to indulge in her old delights while enjoying the praise of her people as well—for the prosperity she has given them in conquering this great land."

Quinn hummed low in her throat as a response.

The scent of black powder hung in the air and cries of violence rose in from the crowd as the opposing crews stormed each other's decks in a clash of swords. Plumes of gray and black smoke lifted to the skies.

"It's an interesting way to celebrate," Quinn finally said as one of Imogen's men swung across the narrow stretch of water, his sword in one hand and the rope clasped tightly in the other. His boots teetered on the edge of the wooden rail of Axe's vessel as he tried and failed to balance, only to be shoved over into the unforgiving waves. A head full of ruby-tinted hair popped up and a hand reached out, grasping the fallen man's rope before it could swing back to Imogen's ship. Axe tightened her fist around the cable and hoisted herself onto the ledge. With a flashing grin she swiftly removed an axe from her belt and jumped—using the side of the blade to knock away an impending attacker as she landed upon the other boat. Quinn blinked as the girl disappeared from view, only to return a moment later as she flipped her attacker over the side, allowing him to join his other crew member in the bay below.

"Imogen reenacts the first week of her battle for

Ilvas," Zorel explained. "With a few caveats, of course."

"Caveats?" Quinn narrowed her eyes. "What do you mean?"

Zorel stared over the bay to the two ships, quiet for a moment before he looked to Quinn and answered with a tight smile. "The Queen is grooming her daughter to take over for her someday, and these battles are part of Axelle's training." He turned back to face the encounter before continuing.

"The Queen believes that in order to rule, Axelle must understand the importance of hard work. She has to have the experience of an earned victory before she can reap the rewards of her reign. She has participated in these battles for the last three years."

Quinn frowned. "She's still a child," she pointed out.

Zorel nodded. "In many ways, yes," he said stiffly. "But the Queen wants her to learn, and there's no better way to teach her daughter than in the midst of cannon-fire and clashing swords."

"So, they're reenacting the first battle for Ilvas, but she expects Axe to win?" Quinn shook her head. She was obviously reckless leaving her own ship behind to infiltrate Imogen's. Brash and audacious enough, it was actually almost predictable. Unless, she intended to be predictable. Quinn tilted her head thoughtfully. Yes, Axe was young, but Quinn had lived long enough to know not to misjudge or assume anything of anyone too early.

"Yes," Zorel said. "The Queen has promised that as soon as Axelle defeats her, she will step down and allow Axelle to rule."

He feigned disinterest at the clashing of vessels across the bay but squinted slightly every time Axe took out an attacker. The wind whipped her shining hair as Axe raised her weapon and let out a battle cry. Quinn watched as his lips thinned and the muscles of his jaw twitched. Zorel didn't care for the Queen's daughter, that much was obvious. Given how Axe had acted the morning they arrived, she wasn't too fond of him either.

A loud boom echoed, startling Quinn. She pivoted sharply and reached back to the railing, as a plume of smoke came pouring out of the side of Axe's ship.

The girl paused mid-fight, her back stiffening before she looked to her own ship. The crew began

diving from the deck as the vessel started to sink—
and with it, her victory.

Quinn narrowed her gaze, searching for the
hole in the wood siding, noting she hadn't heard
another cannon go off.

Not finding one, she glanced away from the
wreckage and back to her side. She blinked when
she realized Zorel was gone. Spinning fully, she
spotted him several paces away. Even as he slunk
away into the crowd, he turned his cheek, and
Quinn caught a glimpse of a small smile.

She took a step in his direction when the crowd
began to move away from the railings and toward
the taverns, already open and booming with business. Bodies jostled her as they tried to move past,
complaining loudly about lost bets as the battle
came to a close and Imogen was pronounced the
victor.

Quinn struggled to find a path out of the
congregation of people, growing more agitated as
the crowd refused to give way. Losing patience, she
sent out a pulse of anxiety, stopping several people
in their tracks. As they paused, trying to find the
source of their newfound unease, she searched for
her way out. The stragglers that had been caught by

her power created a gap just big enough for her to slip through without anyone the wiser. She slid down an alley, watching as the group of men and women shuffled by—some faster than others—the dread they had been feeling dispersed, and their jovial voices once again rose in volume. A head of dark blond hair appeared in the sea of people, moving with a keen agility she knew well enough. Draeven cut through the crowd much easier than Quinn had, his steps purposeful, his gait expeditious.

He was focused. On what, Quinn didn't know. Whatever it was that Draeven had set his sights on, however, was traversing away from him. With a huff, Quinn slipped back into the horde and followed.

Sweat slicked down the back of her neck as the sun rose higher in the sky. She sent an irritated glance upward before cutting across a family of five and striding closer. The bobbing of his head disappeared, and she stopped, cursing herself.

"Quinn." She jerked at the sound, rounding on the direction it came from.

Draeven leaned casually against the outside wall of a building, eyes pinned to her form. She moved closer when the throng of people at her back pressed too close, and he lifted a brow.

"Hey," she said.

He didn't even blink. "Why are you following me?"

"I wasn't," she lied. "I didn't even notice you. What are you doing here?"

Draeven dropped the brow and shook his head. Instead of answering her question, he gestured for her to follow after him. "Come on," he said, turning and heading down the narrow alleyway to his left.

Quinn fell in line behind him as they squeezed through the space between buildings onto a much less crowded cobblestone street. The scent of sulfur pervaded her nostrils, and Quinn rubbed her nose.

"It's from the cannons," Draeven said, peeking back at her. "It'll go away."

She nodded, but otherwise didn't respond as he led her up the hill to the corner shop and around the back. Quinn stopped and frowned as he climbed atop a tall wooden trash box set against the building and reached for the shingles of the roof, curling his fingers over the ledge of the rooftop and hoisting himself up. His front met the clay plates as he grunted, trying to shift upward. Draeven rolled over once he was far enough up the roof and let his legs dangle over the edge as he said, "Are you coming or not?"

Quinn debated asking him what in the dark realm he thought he was doing, but she doubted he would give her a straight answer. With a sigh of frustration, she climbed atop the trash box, giving him a dubious glance when he made no attempt to help her. He cracked a grin, waiting for her to ask. Quinn pursed her lips, bending at the knees as she jumped, grabbing hold of the tiles and heaving herself up, muscles straining as she kept her mouth in a pressed line.

Once the two of them were firmly on the roof, Draeven rose to his feet and started for the next building over that was even higher, but not nearly so hard to scale. Quinn trailed behind him, following his footsteps until they came to a stop. Draeven plopped down harder than she thought necessary, sighing in relief as he leaned back.

"What are we doing here?" she asked.

"Watching the show," he replied, patting the spot next to him.

Quinn watched for a moment more before slowly sliding down—suspicion and wariness keeping her vigilant as she settled in and extended her legs firmly against the shingles' edge. As it was, the roof was steep, and with Draeven's elbows propped, she half expected him to slip right off.

"How can you see anything like that?"

"I can see just fine," he assured her with a dry chuckle. "Don't you worry about me. Why don't you take a look?"

Fires were lit in almost every corner of the city —the smell of roasting meat thick in the air, replacing the earlier scent of black powder. As Draeven had said, already the smell of sulfur was beginning to fade. Men and women alike danced about in drunken glee. It seemed as though the whole of the city had been shut down for this celebration. No shops were open save for the taverns and small stalls in the marketplace plazas. If people weren't yet inebriated, they were well on their way.

"Look at them," Draeven said with a small laugh. He closed his eyes and reclined even further, crossing his arms behind his head with a long exhale. "What a time to be alive, eh?"

"I am looking," Quinn said, clearly missing whatever he saw. "All I see are intoxicated idiots. What else is there to see?"

Draeven's eyes slid open once more and settled on Quinn. "You don't wish to be them?" he asked.

She scowled. "Why would I?"

He watched her curiously. "They have such nice lives, don't you think?" he asked. "I envy their freedom. To live and laugh and love as they do. To not be bound by the gods as we are in the ways that we are." An ominous cloud seemed to settle over his features, something that intrigued Quinn. But it was only there for a moment before it disappeared, and he smiled her way with an ease that she was beginning to wonder about. "Wouldn't it be sweet for life to be as simple as enjoying a holiday with a few spirits?"

Quinn frowned. "Life is rarely as simple as drunkards believe it to be."

"Ah, but that's just the spirits talking," he replied with a smirk. "Spirits have a way of driving out the madness in a soul, if only for a little while. Sometimes I wonder what it would be like if we didn't need spirits to drive anything out. If we could do it just by asking them to leave."

"Wonder away," Quinn said. "But wishing for dreams to come true rarely does anything but produce false hopes. Once spirits desert you and reality comes back, it's all the more disappointing to know it was only a fantasy."

"It's unfortunate," he said, a grievous sigh slipping from between his lips, causing her to narrow her gaze on him. "You're so pessimistic."

"I prefer realistic," Quinn huffed.

He smirked. "Prefer all you like, doesn't change the facts."

She watched the people dancing in their drunken stupors for a while longer as they sat there on the roof without saying anything to each other. There was a comfortable sort of silence between them. It lacked the tension that Lazarus created whenever he was near, nor was there a heavy feeling —like a weight on her chest—that she felt around Lorraine. With Draeven, neither of them particularly cared for each other, but they made it work all the same, and it was easier for it.

"You ran out rather quickly the other night," she said, breaking the silence.

Draeven's shoulders stiffened for a moment before he forced himself to relax. "I was tired," he replied lightly before adding with a smirk, "How was your talk with Lazarus?"

Quinn's lips twitched. "Interesting."

"Oh?" He rolled to his side, propping his head up with an elbow planted upon the rooftop. "How so?" He waited, and Quinn shook her head at him, stretching her own legs out along the shingles beneath them.

"He showed me his mark."

Draeven glanced over at her out of the corner of his eye. "He did?" The question was stated, though Quinn could tell he didn't really expect an answer. It simply slid out as though he couldn't help himself.

She nodded solemnly. "I imagine you've seen it as well?" she asked.

Draeven twisted and let his back hit the rooftop once more, this time with a harder thump. He grunted upon impact and sucked in a deep breath. "I have."

She wanted for him to say more, and when he didn't, she pressed him. "What he's doing is a bit reckless, don't you think?"

"I'm afraid I don't know what you mean." Draeven let his eyes slide shut, the tone of his voice even, indifferent. Quinn's lips twitched down in a frown.

"If you've seen his mark as you say you have, then surely—"

"Lazarus will do whatever Lazarus will do," he interrupted her. "Neither I, nor you, nor anyone out there can stop him once his mind is set." Draeven's eyes opened once more, and he canted his head to the side. Their gazes met and held for a brief moment in time. She realized he knew exactly what she had been talking about. The way the souls beneath Lazarus' skin ate away at the marking etched into his chest. "It's useless," Draeven whispered. "There's nothing that can be done to change him or his mind."

Whether that was true or not, Quinn didn't care for the implications. Draeven turned his head away and stared up into the vastness of the sky as Leviticus' eye sank under the brilliant colors its descent spilled on the horizon. There they sat in the twilight, above the streets filled with Ilvan citizens. Time crawled by, stretched further by the silence between them. Quinn's concentration slipped from person to person. A plump middle-aged woman in a stained apron dancing with a much younger man. A skinny weed of a child darting between people, hands reaching out, grasping at things dangling from pockets. A slender young maid with blonde curls shyly accepting a drink from a man of considerable height, but similar age. Quinn watched all of this with an unknown feeling settling in her chest; one she was unaccustomed to. She began to grow restless.

"Why are we up here?" she asked after a while.

Draeven shrugged. "Why not?"

Quinn growled low beneath her breath; frustration evident. "If you won't tell me why we're here, will you say who you were trailing before you caught me?"

"I thought you said you weren't following me," he replied lazily.

Quinn rolled her eyes. "Why are you evading my questions?" she demanded.

His shoulders tightening, his jaw flexed for a moment before he breathed out and released the tension. "It doesn't matter who I was trailing," he finally said, giving Quinn her much desired answer. "I've lost them for the time being."

Quinn didn't have a reply. She still wanted to know who it was that he had been following, but she doubted he would say without a much more persuasive approach. Lazarus likely wouldn't appreciate any lasting damage to his left-hand.

Her focus cut back to the streets below. It appeared as if more drink had been added to the rambunctious mixture of people below. Some of the younger men had thrown off their shirts and stood together in nothing but their skivvies and trousers. Across the way, one particularly drunken man thought it might be a good idea to attempt climbing the side of the building. He got about halfway up before losing his footing and slipping back down to the bottom. There was a brief moment of stunned silence around him as he landed on his back against the hard ground, but the absence of any broken bones and serious injuries had his friends howling in amusement. Quinn watched, partly fascinated and partly irked by the scene, as the man got up and brushed against his scrapes and bruises as someone handed him a mug of spirits, and he downed it with a smile.

Easy, she thought. *An easy existence these creatures live every day.* It wasn't something she had ever had the luxury of.

"You said you wished to be like these people," Quinn found herself saying.

Draeven hummed at the interruption to his peaceful quiet before grumbling out a half-hearted, "So I did."

"Maybe you're right." The thoughtful admission drew the brunt of Draeven's attention back to her as he swung his eyes her way.

"Right about what, exactly?" he asked.

"Maybe their easy lives would be nice," she said. "But that's not who I am. I cannot simply take a life that is not my own and pretend to be a person that I'm not." She shook her head. "Besides, that's not what I want."

He considered that for a moment and finally said, "I never called their lives 'easy'. I said that it would be nice to have a simplistic life."

Quinn frowned and gestured out to the crowds. "How are their lives *not* easy?" she asked. "Look at them. They do not struggle as we struggle. The world ignores them for the most part, leaves them to lead their lives however they wish." As she spoke the words, Quinn felt the fingers of her right hand gently touch the wrist of her left. Though they were long gone, burned away by a concoction that had scalded her skin clean, the brands of her old slave masters were a silent, invisible reminder of what she had been.

Unaware of Quinn's internal struggle, Draeven shrugged again before he sat up and crossed his legs. "Easy is relative. What is easy for one isn't for another."

"You're saying their lives aren't easy, then?" Quinn asked in disbelief, dropping her fingers away from her wrist. "All they do is drink and work. Eat and sleep. Fuck and breed. They're like animals. Simple and dumb. They would hardly know what to do if their whole world was flipped on its head or, Gods forbid, a war were to befall them." The hint of sarcastic irritation in her final words wasn't masked.

Draeven shook his head. "I don't think you're seeing them clearly," he argued. "Look again."

Quinn gritted her teeth and turned back to the crowds. There again, men and women dancing, kissing, embracing each other—out in the open. It made her scowl deepen as she was reminded of Lazarus. They were not to do these things in the light of day, but only hidden in the shadows of night. They—she and Lazarus—were creatures of darkness, fueled by vengeance and power. But these people, they were not like her. They were not like Lazarus.

She and Lazarus were separate from these creatures that drank in the night and basked in the sun. If anything, Draeven was closer to them than she. Quinn inhaled sharply. "Whether their lives are easy and simple, or hard and unforgiving," she said, "they are sheep. And I," she paused, turning to meet Draeven's eyes once more, "am a wolf."

Draeven didn't reply as Quinn stood and made her way back across the rooftop, leaving him behind as she climbed down and headed back to the Queen's palace.

Casual touches, soft light, and peals of laughter . . . the sights and sounds haunted her in its own right because those kinds of things weren't meant for monsters like her.

She was a creature of the dark, and she was content to stay that way.

Virulent Garden

"There's no such thing as coincidences, only untimely accidents."
— Quinn Darkova, vassal of House Fierté, fear twister

Beams of light streamed in through the palace windows, illuminating the cracks in the marbled floors as Quinn's boots clomped against them with each step. Tritol was quiet in the early morning after the drunks had all gone home or passed out in the streets beyond. Not a soul was in sight, nor a sound heard beyond the wind and the ocean waves. She slowed to a stop and raised her fist to knock when the heavy wooden door swung open.

Quinn frowned down at the pile of blankets being shoved toward her and the salt-and-peppered hair that just barely peeked over the mound. The healer Magi started forward, running straight into Quinn before falling back. The woman craned her neck, trying to search for what had stopped her forward momentum.

Quinn shook her head and sighed. "I'm looking for Lorraine."

The other woman grumbled under her breath in Ilvan—something about entitled Norcastans—before shifting the laundry pile to one side and bringing her short arm up to hook her thumb to the side, motioning down the hall. "That way," the healer said, switching to broken Norcastan.

"Thank you," Quinn murmured with a nod, turning for the direction she motioned. A soft, sensual laughter caught her attention, just as she came to a stop in front of an archway. Beyond was a garden, lush in greenery and well-groomed. It housed a small wooden table and two chairs. Seated there was Lorraine, laughing lightly as she leaned forward into none other than Dominicus.

Quinn paused and leaned against the stone

arch, arms crossed over her chest while she watched them together.

"You're pushing yourself too hard, Raine—"

"I've lived through far worse things to let an arrow keep me down." She smiled through the pain, and Quinn wondered if Dominicus saw it as easily as she did. "Besides, I love this garden. It reminds me of home. We have trees just like this at Shallowyn."

He smiled at her, and it was tender but also sad as he reached forward to clasp her fingers in his. A light blush crept up Lorraine's cheeks, and Quinn leaned forward, her brows drawn.

"E'scuse me, Miss," came a voice behind her. Quinn blinked and glanced back to see a young woman holding a tray with teacups, motioning toward the garden. Quinn stepped to the side and turned back to see both Dominicus and Lorraine staring.

"What are you doing here?" he asked her. Quinn bristled in response.

"I was coming to check on Lorraine, and the healer said she was out here," she answered defensively. Quinn paused as if to wait for Dominicus to reply or Lorraine to say something, and when neither of them did, she continued. "Well, if I inter-rupted something—"

"You did."

"—then I might as well stay." They both fell silent. Dominicus shot her a withering glare, and Quinn grinned, unphased by his dislike. Lorraine let out a slight chuckle that turned into a cough, and the tea girl rushed forward.

"Here, drink this," the woman said in Norcas-tan. She set two cups down and waited for Lorraine to start sipping before she turned to leave.

"Come join us, Quinn," Lorraine offered, sighing happily as she set the cup down and settled back in her chair.

Quinn strode forward, glancing between the two seats as she came to a stop between them. Dominicus' jaw twitched as he pointedly watched her, and she obtusely ignored him.

"Are you sure you're well enough to be out here?" Quinn asked her. A flicker of something foreign spread through her chest as she took in the ashen pallor of the older woman's normally tan skin. Hair that usually appeared thick and well-managed despite the elements was stringy and unwashed. Lorraine lifted the cup to her lips again, and the liquid trembled as her fingers shook slightly.

Quinn lifted an eyebrow, and Lorraine sighed again. Softly. Wearily.

She was tired and hurting more than she wanted to let on.

"In this, the girl's right. You really shouldn't—" Dominicus started. Lorraine held up her hand, then closed it in a fist as her fingers shook more.

"Dom, could you go tell Harrietta that I'd like a bath drawn, please?" she asked him, leaning forward to place that sweaty hand over his. She gave him a sweet smile that Dominicus was hopeless to refuse.

"Alright, Raine." He moved to stand, his eyes shifting from her to Quinn. He opened his mouth to say something when Lorraine spoke again.

"Could you ask her to put some extra epsom in it? It numbs the sutures."

He stood there for a moment, conveying his displeasure with his eyes as he stared at Quinn, and she returned it with no small amount of disinterest.

"Of course, I'll be *right* back," he replied before striding out, emphasizing his intent for a quick return. Quinn took the now empty seat and glanced back at Lorraine, that odd sensation filling her chest again.

"What happened wasn't your fault, Quinn," the

old woman said suddenly. The sugared tone she used with Dominicus dissolved as she breathed deeply, letting how unwell she actually was show. "Stop feeling guilty."

"Guilty?" Quinn repeated. "I don't—"

"It's the eyes," Lorraine interrupted softly. She took another sip of her tea, and despite her state, the eyes that gave Quinn an appraising scan were clear. Sharp. "You're unapologetic about most everything you do, but you look at me like I'm broken and you're the cause. I'm not, and neither are you."

Quinn wasn't sure what to make of this unusually forward Lorraine. She wasn't sure if she liked it, especially not when she knew it was the pain causing it. It almost made her miss Lady Manners. *Almost*.

"You're not well, but you're sitting out here drinking tea like you are," Quinn said. "Why?"

Lorraine chuckled once and then swallowed, her head tilting back to stare up at the trees. "I wasn't lying when I said I've been through worse things. I might not be a Maji, but I'm resilient. It'll take a lot to keep me from making it back to my son." Quinn frowned at the turn in conversation and glanced down at the new untouched cup the girl had brought for Dominicus. Quinn leaned forward and took a whiff. Lemon, rosemary, and verbena along with something else. She shrugged to herself, and took the delicate handle between three fingers, lifting it to her lips. The hot liquid was remarkably soothing and the taste sweet, but not unpleasantly so.

"You don't talk about your son much," Quinn said, letting Lorraine decide how much or how little she wanted to say.

"I don't know much," Lorraine replied. "He was a boy when Lazarus granted us asylum, and still a child when I sent him away to school. He's almost grown now, and I know very little about the man he's become."

"You don't sound bitter about it." Quinn swished the liquid in the cup as she held it. "But sad. If you didn't want to send him away, then why did you?" She glanced up to find Lorraine staring at her. Not with anger, or frustration, or even defensiveness. The look on her face was unreadable, even to Quinn. They stared at each other for several long moments, and just when Quinn turned to get up because she thought she wouldn't answer, Lorraine spoke.

"Sometimes, we have to make sacrifices for the

people we love. I was newly employed and without a husband or help when Lazarus offered to pay for my son to get the best education gold could buy." Lorraine smiled wistfully. "I had two choices, Quinn. I could raise him, knowing he would never amount to more than myself . . ." Lorraine paused, taking a slight, shuddering breath. "Or I could send him away and miss his childhood, but he'd be as educated and capable as any noble—and with Master Lazarus becoming king, one day he might actually be one."

Quinn's lips parted as she took that in. "You gave up everything for him."

"Not quite," Lorraine said. "Both my boy and I have lived good lives. I missed his youth, but if I had the choice to do it over again—I wouldn't change a thing. I've sacrificed much for my son, but I'm truly happy to do the work I do for Master Lazarus. I'm thankful for the life he's given us and the things I've gotten to experience because of him."

"You feel that way even though you could have died from that arrow?" Quinn asked, not judging or disbelieving, but curious.

"Dear, that's not the first attempt on my life I've faced since I became a vassal of House Fierté—and it won't be the last." Lorraine gave her a slight smile that said a lot about the woman Quinn was only just beginning to see. "Lazarus gives much because he asks much. I have no disillusions about my choice of profession."

"You know, I wasn't sure that you actually understood the kind of person you were working for —or much about the world at all—when we met. There's more to you than you let on," Quinn stated, settling back in her chair. She placed her cup back on the table and relished the slight breeze under the shaded canopy of the garden.

"People aren't stagnant, Quinn. There's always more beneath the surface, but you need to earn the right to see it." Lorraine gave her an amused grin as she gripped the teacup too tight between her thin fingers. The muscles of her hand spasmed, and Lorraine stilled.

"I know you told Dominicus you're fine, but you don't have to lie to me—" Quinn's words broke off as the teacup tilted sideways. Glass met wood and the cup cracked, spilling liquid everywhere. The beautiful scene shattered as the tiny pink blossoms that had fallen on the table floated in the amber liquid as it pooled, spilling over the sides.

Lorraine jerked, her eyes going wide for a

moment before sagging. She looked up once more, past Quinn. "The flowers . . ." she breathed, almost like she was taking them in for the last time. Quinn swallowed and glanced to the archway, but no one was there, and the city was drunk or sleeping.

Lorraine's eyes slid closed as she fell from her chair and into the autumn leaves that had gathered on the stone pathway next to them. Her shoulders shuddered as her muscles spasmed.

Quinn jerked her head back as her eyes widened. A heaviness settled on her chest once more as her heartbeat began to race. Blood pounded in Quinn's ears as she tried to process what was happening.

"Help!" Quinn shouted, but no one came. "*Potes*," she cursed. "She's dying, we need help!" Impatient and feeling the time slip away, she bolted to her feet and did the only thing she could—she wasn't even completely sure how she managed it, but her magic drove forward anyway.

A flare of panic rose up, and Quinn sent it out. The sharp wave would cover Tritol, if only for a moment, and in that brief lapse of time where her magic came alive and Lorraine lay dying, Quinn felt a responding answer from the other side of the palace.

Capricious Circumstances

"Sometimes the difference between want and need is a scarcely thin line and copious amounts of willpower."
— *Lazarus Fierté, soul eater, heir to Norcasta, mercurial prince*

Lazarus froze, his muscles tensing as a shockwave of anxiety slammed into him. His heart thrummed heavily, beating hard against his chest as though it were trying to break free from the cage of bone. Sweat beaded along his forehead and down the center of his back. Next to him, Draeven stumbled and only a palm to the wall kept Lazarus' left-hand on his feet.

"What in the bloody dark realm was *that?*" Draeven demanded, scanning behind him as though the wave had been a physical blow from a man he could fight instead of a mere brush with fear itself.

"Something's wrong with Quinn," Lazarus said, attempting to sense where exactly the wave had come from; which direction he was now meant to go. When several gasps of shock echoed from down the corridor, Lazarus turned south and sent a responding rush of his own power out. An answer to her call. He was coming.

"Where are you going?" Draeven asked as Lazarus began to stalk down the corridor. He weaved through masses of hysterical people as they stumbled from their rooms into the passageway, shoving several aside as Draeven rushed to catch up.

There was a savage need to find her, a pull that he couldn't resist as it faintly guided him to that beacon of dark power in the sea of ordinary.

He turned the corner of a stone archway, readying himself to fight—to kill—but the scene was not what he expected. Quinn stood, silent and weary, as two palace guards and the healer helped to hurry an unconscious Lorraine back to her room.

"What happened?" Lazarus demanded.

Quinn was slow to react, almost sluggish. She shook her head, as if shaking the feeling from her mind, and responded, "I don't know. She just . . . collapsed."

Draeven came to a stop beside him, silently taking in the corridor and the garden with a single sweep. "This isn't going to be good," his left-hand said. Lazarus stiffened as the words had barely been spoken when another man came into his direct view.

Dominicus rushed down the hallway, his fists clenched, and his steps hurried. Lazarus stepped in front of Quinn just as the weapons master reached them—homing in on her with the same uncanny focus that made him good at his work, and Quinn took notice as she stepped to the side, back around him. Lazarus growled, but she simply shrugged it off with an aloofness that only she could manage.

"I left Lorraine alone with you and this is what I come back to? What did you do?" Dominicus demanded.

"She collapsed," Quinn repeated, her attention straying toward the garden.

"How?" Dominicus asked.

Her lips pinched together, turning colorless. "I

don't know," she snapped. "We were talking. She said something about the flowers, and then she fainted."

Dominicus' eyes narrowed on her. "What were you talking about?"

Quinn stiffened. "What we talk about is none of your concern."

Dominicus bristled. He opened his mouth to speak but was interrupted when Harrietta came back and his attention was diverted. "How is she?" he asked.

The healer blinked at him and then turned to Lazarus. With her stilted, broken Norcastan, she attempted to relay information on Lorraine's condition. "Fall opened wound," she stated, motioning to her stomach region to mimic where Lorraine's injury was. "Too early be out of bed. Will rest for now."

Lazarus nodded as if that was all he needed to know. Dominicus' shoulders sagged in relief, but as soon as the healer turned her back on them to leave, his eyes snapped open. Shadows stirred there. Fire and ash. While his weapons master wasn't the most well-tempered of his vassals, he certainly wasn't the worst.

Lazarus glanced between the two of them,

taking in the rising tensions as Dominicus' affections for Lorraine coupled with his fear of Quinn's power. His reactionary response could send Quinn into a rage, and that wouldn't end well for any of them. He needed to diffuse the situation before he truly provoked her, and they had a very real problem on their hands.

"Go," Lazarus said with a sigh, gesturing beyond toward the infirmary. "Watch over her."

Dominicus gave a slow direct nod, his body already turning to start toward Lorraine, though his glare stayed set on Quinn. The expression she wore was an apathetic mask that unsettled Lazarus more than Lorraine's actual injury or her fall.

"Stay with him," Lazarus said as he nodded to Draeven. "And if you can find the mountain boy, I want someone to keep track of him as well."

Draeven nodded and trailed after Dominicus as they headed for Lorraine's healing chamber, leaving Lazarus and Quinn completely alone.

"Now," he said, pausing to take in the flash of something wicked that peeked out from behind her impassive mask for only a moment, before she went expressionless again. "Tell me everything exactly as it happened."

"Lorraine and I were talking," she started with a

sigh, "and she froze for a moment, then said something about the flowers—" Quinn stopped, and her eyes darted toward the garden.

Lazarus' followed her stare, stepping farther inside the lush greenery and away from the heady scent of her dark power. Despite the urgency of the situation and the concern he had for Lorraine, having Quinn so close still set him on edge—the whispers beneath his flesh squirming to get out, urging him to move closer.

He grit his teeth as he scanned the area—noting the familiar petals and skimming to the shattered teacup and the slight smudge of blood on the stone beneath his feet.

"Did she say anything else?" he inquired, his eyes scanning the nearby area.

Quinn hesitated before shaking her head. "She was in pain, but I didn't think much of it because it's expected that she would be."

Lazarus darted his eyes back to Quinn as she lingered at the entrance to the garden. She appeared quieter than usual. When Dominicus had been so unusually abrupt with her, instead of biting back, she chose to go cold. The emotion didn't sit well with him. Not where she was concerned.

"What's wrong?" Lazarus asked.

Quinn lifted her head. "What do you mean what's wrong?" she asked. "Lorraine reopened her wound."

"That's not what I meant." Lazarus shifted closer to her, knowing how his souls would react and yet unable to help himself. Unable to stop.

"Then I don't know what you mean."

Lazarus stepped through the entrance right alongside Quinn's position and eyed her. She remained stationary, glaring up at him for a brief moment before she turned her gaze away, letting it trail back to the gardens, to the exact place where Lorraine had fallen, he suspected. "Tell me about Lorraine," Lazarus said, instead of pressing her for more information she wasn't willing to give. "I want every detail no matter how minor you think it could be."

"Like I said before"—the tone of Quinn's voice suggested she didn't appreciate having to repeat herself so many times—"we weren't doing anything but sitting there." Her eyes locked firmly on the ground. "We were just talking."

"What were you talking about?" Lazarus asked.

Quinn stiffened, and it was then that Lazarus recalled her reaction to Dominicus asking her the same thing. He half expected a similar volatile response, but it never came. Instead, she sucked in a breath and released it as if forcing all of the tension away to focus on his question and the answers he required of her.

"We talked about people," she admitted. "Dominicus . . . herself . . ."

Lazarus waited patiently. He knew what she would not say. Lorraine was steadfast in her loyalty to him, and Quinn was not yet completely trusting. The older stewardess had likely been singing his praises in the hopes that Quinn might loosen up. Lazarus shook his head, knowing the woman meant well, but nothing would convince Quinn other than his actions. Until he had proved himself to her, she would remain cautious. He often wondered if the N'skari woman would ever find him worthy of her devotion and trust.

"And just before she collapsed?" he pressed.

"She was drinking her tea. She'd only taken a sip . . ." Quinn paused, a frown marring her face and twisting the concern there into thoughtfulness. Lazarus sighed when she didn't continue. He looked up toward the open roof of the gardens and into the sky above where seagulls circled overhead, shrieking out their cries and darting back toward the bay.

"Quinn." Lazarus reached out, gripping Quinn's chin, turning her to face him, demanding her attention.

"What are you doing?" she snapped as Lazarus leaned forward. Quinn scowled at him, nearly jerking her face away the closer he came, but he held her steady and firm in his grasp.

"Lorraine will be taken care of," he said, "but in the future, I would appreciate it if you did not antagonize my weapons master as much."

"Antagonize him?" Quinn shoved back, and Lazarus let her go without argument. "You should tell that to him. I do not appreciate his implied accusations simply because he doesn't like me."

"You know that's not why," Lazarus said.

Quinn's eyes dilated. "It's because he fears me," she snapped and then grinned. "Good."

Lazarus fixed her with a focused glare. "You understand that not all fear is entirely logical. Let it go for now. If he presses, do not respond."

Silence echoed between them, and Lazarus' eyes narrowed as Quinn's snarl slipped away and was replaced by a cruel twist of her lips. "You know as well as I, Lazarus, that his fear of me is entirely logical. After what he saw . . . what you all saw, I am not surprised by it. What surprises me is that neither Lorraine nor Draeven seem to have the same reaction to me."

"Draeven and Lorraine understand the Maji power far more than Dominicus. As a non-Maji, he does not possess the same intricate knowledge of the extent of our abilities. He is good at what he does, but you must give him some latitude. He is my vassal, just as you are. I demand that you, at the very least, attempt to tolerate each other."

Quinn huffed and turned away. "Contrary to what you might think, the world doesn't revolve around you." She said it mockingly, her voice holding more than a small trace of caustic irritation.

"What is that supposed to mean?" he demanded.

Quinn rolled her eyes. "It means," she started, "that the emotions of your vassals cannot be controlled just because you will it so. I will do my part, but I cannot change Dominicus' fear of me. Fear will continue to make him act as he does, no matter what you say."

Lazarus frowned. He couldn't deny the legitimacy of her claim, and it rankled him. Her icy blue eyes bored into him as she pivoted once more and faced him head on. Finally, with a resigned breath, he gave her a nod. "I will have a discussion with him," he finally conceded. "That will do." After a beat, simply because he could not help himself, he returned her harsh stare with one of his own and added, "For now."

Quinn didn't respond immediately, but when she did, it was to attempt to brush by him. "I suppose we're done talking, then," she said absently.

Lazarus chuckled under his breath. Quinn paused at the noise, when Lazarus reached out and snatched her, turning her and pushing until her spine was flush against the entrance to the gardens. He loomed before her.

"I don't think so," he said.

"Oh?" Quinn lifted her hand and patted her open mouth as she mimed a yawn. "Was there something else you wanted to discuss? Perhaps you want to blame me for someone else's emotions as well?"

"You are not the only one I scold, Quinn," he said. The woman he had trapped between himself and the wall didn't act as though she was trapped. Quinn lounged back against the stone, staring up at him. "I told you I would talk with him."

She rolled her eyes. "Don't bother." Quinn reached for his arm, meaning to duck beneath and stride off once more, but he stopped her with a shift of his hips, and she froze. Anger echoed across her face; so unique, so fascinating. Lazarus found himself transfixed by the violence in her. "Release me, Lazarus," she said through gritted teeth. "I'm far too busy performing my *vassal duties*"—she spat the words as if they were distasteful to her—"to cater to your every whim and desire."

Lazarus' eyes flashed, and his nostrils flared as every muscle in his body tightened against the thinly veiled insult. "As my vassal, it *is* your duty to cater to my every whim and desire," he growled.

Quinn's lips thinned. "I'm not in the mood for this game, Lazarus."

"There is no game." His voice was a rumble; a slow, deep sound of thunder emitting from his throat.

Her cerulean eyes bored into him. "There is always a game with you. First, we were talking of Lorraine and Dominicus, and now you have me pressed to the wall. Everything you do is a game. You kiss me and then you treat me as though I'm simply another servant among your horde. You've made your refusal quite clear, and vassal or not, I do not beg men for their attentions."

"No, of course not," Lazarus said slowly. He

ran his eyes over her, noting her stiff muscles and damning lips. "You have far too much pride for that."

"Then release me," she snapped.

His lips twitched at the ire of her words, the growing fire within her eyes. Lazarus shook his head. "Why would I do that?" he inquired absently. The souls beneath his skin shivered in delight, moving beneath his flesh to each part of him that pressed against her. Those damned souls—more than anything else—kept him right where he was when he knew it would have been smarter to release the woman and step away; to let her go as she wanted to. But her intense desire to leave his presence was just as much a reason to keep her right where she was. If only to show her who was actually in command.

Quinn glared at him for a moment more before her frown eased away and something else entered her expression, causing him to frown this time. "I have other things to worry about that don't involve you, Lazarus."

Quinn shifted forward, rubbing against him. She angled her hips inwardly to rock into his, and he stiffened. Lazarus lifted an impassive eyebrow, masking his emotions.

"Unless . . ." she continued, speaking in a breathless and husky voice. "You wanted to pick up where we left off the last time we were this close. I'm not all about pleasing *my lord*, but if my lord wanted to please *me* . . . well, I could make an exception. Just once, I suppose."

"You avoid me," Lazarus accused through gritted teeth as the sound of her voice and her suggested words sent a rush of pleasure straight to his groin.

She shrugged. "I'm not avoiding you. You're here, aren't you?" she pointed out. "Much as I'd prefer you to be on a horse heading straight for the dark realm, you're the one who has *me* against a wall."

Lazarus released her abruptly and backed off. With a wayward grin on her lips, Quinn side-stepped around him. Before he could turn and say anything, she made a sound of amusement in the back of her throat. Lazarus jerked his gaze over his shoulder and an immediate glower overtook him. Vaughn was striding toward them, eyes set on Quinn as he approached.

"She-wolf Quinn," he said by way of greeting. The oversized mountain boy flicked a glance

Lazarus' way but made no move to greet him as well.

"Vaughn." She smiled; her eyes fixed on him. Lazarus' teeth threatened to crack under the strain of his clenched jaw.

"There is training yard," he said, his speech still lacking in refinement, though he had already learned a decent bit over the last few weeks. "Will you join?"

Quinn took one look back over her shoulder at Lazarus and nodded. A glint of something vicious settled in her gaze as she said, "Of course."

The boy must not have cared too greatly for his life because he offered his arm to Quinn and she, being Quinn, didn't seem to comprehend the gravity of the situation because she took it.

As they started to stride away, Lazarus considered how truly important his alliance with Thorne was before Quinn paused.

"I'll come by to check on Lorraine," she said over her shoulder, her voice going a shade darker as she added, "I'm sure Dominicus will be there, but I won't be a *hindrance*."

With that, she left, and Lazarus wasn't sure what to call the strange feeling sliding through him, though he'd felt it before—and now he felt it each time the boy came near her. The souls beneath his skin writhed with need because for the first time in all his life—he wanted a woman he shouldn't have.

Quinn was violent and unpredictable. She was prone to fits of madness and rage.

She was not a good choice to warm his bed when he was going to be king.

She was too irrational. Too . . . territorial.

Then again, so was he.

Queen of Evasion

"You should know as much about your friends as you do your enemies."
— *Quinn Darkova, vassal of House Fierté, fear twister*

D arkness descended over Tritol as Leviticus' eye slipped under the horizon, making way for Leviathan to rise once again. Quinn leaned her arms against the railing, watching the city of drunks, as she liked to call it, with a keen eye. The Pirate Queen's holiday was coming to an end, and with it, Quinn's patience. Though much still remained unfinished, she was ready to leave Ilvas.

Lorraine hadn't recovered from the exertion

that caused a tear in her wound. Whatever danger had befell her that day in the garden still held her under. She was alive but not well. They continued to keep a very close watch on her and would until she woke from the stupor she'd remained in the last two days. At the thought of the other woman, Quinn spared a glance over her shoulder to Dominicus. The weapons master's pacing was putting them all on edge.

Dominicus' unsettling irritation, Lorraine's fallen health, and the fact that the Queen had still refused Lazarus an audience—it appeared as though their departure wouldn't be happening anytime soon, much to Lazarus' great frustration, if the man's glowering was anything to go by.

"Have you tried sending gifts?" Draeven asked from his spot on the lounge. "Women love gifts." He reclined back, smirking at Quinn as he tossed grapes into his mouth. Lazarus sighed and continued sipping his spirits from a glass while staring at the fireplace, like the flames might hold some answers that only he could see.

"I had two chests of gold brought to her before we even reached the Cisean mountains," Lazarus grumbled. "Not to mention the jewelry we found in the market that you had me send this week." He continued pondering a moment longer.

"I'm not sure what to tell you then, Lazarus." Draeven glanced past him toward Dominicus. "Perhaps your weapons master might have some suggestions, given that he earned Lorraine's affections—"

"Do you find yourself funny?" Dominicus asked, shooting him a withering glare.

"Quite often," Draeven responded dryly. Dominicus shook his head and walked out the room, closing the door to his suite hard enough that the furniture rattled.

"He's a moody one. Perhaps our dear Dominicus isn't the most well-suited for advising here. Both he and Lorraine are a bit more stoic than the Pirate Queen." Draeven turned his head again, catching Quinn's eye. He flashed a satisfied grin that said he knew exactly what he was doing. Gone was the brooding male from the previous week and in his place was the same, albeit slightly more amusing, left-hand. "What about you, Vaughn? What would you do to gain an audience with the Queen?"

Vaughn glanced up from the corner of the room, both hands stilling against the greywood spear he was carving as he considered the question. "Bring Queen fruit of the red dawn and behead her enemies," he finally said. His lips pinched together for a moment as if he were contemplating a more elaborate answer, then he nodded once before returning to his spear.

"Uh huh . . ." Draeven drawled, glancing back to Quinn.

"I'm with him," Quinn answered with a shrug before he could even ask.

"You can't be serious," Draeven deadpanned. "You'd rather a man bring you fruit and severed heads over gold and jewelry?" The space between his brows puckered in disbelief.

Quinn turned from the railing and crossed her arms over her chest, leaning against the wooden frame of the open double doors. "The fruit of the red dawn is rare. Exotic." Quinn paused, raising both eyebrows when Draeven opened his mouth to interrupt. He promptly closed it again. "And furthermore, it's a food that Vaughn's people value more than gold or jewels. It's considered a great honor for the Ciseans to gift it to you at a meal, something not even we—who are allied with them —were given the pleasure of." Draeven tilted his head, seeming to consider this.

"But it's just fruit," Draeven said.

"And jewelry is just a useless trinket that women wear to display wealth," Quinn countered. "At least Vaughn's idea of a gift is thoughtful. I'd be more inclined to trust a man who was willing to kill my enemies just as he would his own, than someone that tried to buy my allegiance."

"I can't believe I'm listening to this." Draeven shook his head. "You'd *really* rather someone who killed your enemies and brought you fruit?" Quinn nodded, taking note of how quiet Lazarus had gotten.

"I don't know about these women you keep picking up, Lazarus," Draeven said. "Their priorities just aren't right."

Quinn rolled her eyes and strode toward the door. "If that's all, I'm going to check on Lorraine. The healer said she should wake any day now." Quinn reached for the door, her fingers only just brushing over the cool handle when two thumps from the other side made her pause.

Quinn frowned, and Draeven called, "Don't just stand there. Open the door." Gritting her teeth to bite back a sharp reply, Quinn grasped the handle and pulled, stepping to the side as she did so.

"What do you want?" she asked.

A mop of red hair with beads and feathers swished as Axe strode in. She perused the room with leisure, watching Draeven then Vaughn and finally Lazarus, before turning back to Quinn.

"Another plum liquor, but Aunt Petra cut me off now that *Madara's* holiday is comin' to an end," she bemoaned. "Apparently, I have to go back to my court duties as the princess."

Quinn shook her head and stepped around the girl who stood a full head shorter than her. "Well, if that's all . . ."

"Not so fast," Axe said. Quinn paused in the doorway. "*Madara* sent me because she's decided to grant you an audience."

Quinn frowned, shuffling forward as Lazarus said, "Excellent."

His hulking form drew closer, and Axe coughed. "Not you."

A short pause followed as the pieces clicked together.

She couldn't mean . . .

"*Madara* has decided to grant *you* an audience," Axe said, pointing at Quinn. "Not the rest of them."

"What?" Lazarus asked, a tint of anger entering

his voice. Quinn schooled her face in a mask of neutrality.

"Why would she do that?" Quinn asked, standing with her arms crossed in front of Lazarus.

"How would I know?" Axe shrugged. "She told me that dependin' on what you have to say, she may decide to grant Lord Fierté an audience as well."

Quinn blinked. *Not good*, she thought, right as Draeven said, "We are so screwed."

Quinn pushed her lips together and stared past Axe to the smoldering coals boring down on her. Lazarus' stare was heady and tense with a burnishing intensity so hot she felt her skin heat.

"Are you just goin' to stand there eye-fuckin' each other?" Axe asked in a completely serious tone. Quinn blinked as Draeven choked on a grape and let out a spluttering cough, his fisted hand pounding against his chest as he fought off asphyxiation.

"I'm waiting for you," Quinn answered smoothly, still feeling his eyes on her despite Axe's words. The girl saw both too much and too little.

"Uh huh." Axe snorted, obviously not believing Quinn for a moment. The girl stepped around her and headed for the door. "Sure you were." Axe disappeared into the hallway, muttering something about hussies being coy.

Quinn frowned, but chose to not comment as she followed her out, shooting one last look Lazarus' way. His dark burning stare held a weighted meaning. They would be talking again very soon. Quinn passed through the door, letting it swing shut behind her, and then trailed behind Axe as the smaller girl shook her head and led Quinn off.

Quinn followed behind Axe as they strode through the cracked marble halls, passing servants and guards on the way—all of whom made it a point to steer clear of Axe. The twin arching doors into the throne room were hanging slightly ajar when they arrived. Instead of knocking or announcing her presence, Axe pushed until there was just enough space for both her and Quinn to squeeze through.

Imogen looked up from her chaise lounge, stiff parchment clutched in her hand. She sighed and waved a servant away after shoving the papers into his chest. "Make sure to deliver that to my council," she commanded sharply. The wide-eyed servant nodded and abruptly turned, rushing away as if whatever he held was of the utmost importance. Or perhaps, he didn't want to keep Imogen's orders waiting. Given her reputation of impatience, Quinn could understand the urgency on his part.

Axe bounded up the stairs to her mother's throne, but Imogen shook her head, and Axe froze. "Not today, *Tesora*," she said. "I'd like to talk with Fierté's vassal alone."

Axe's forehead scrunched as her eyebrows drew together. She paused, nodding once before turning on her heel and heading out the side door—tossing a confused glance over her shoulder as she went. Once the doors closed behind her and they were alone, the Queen rose from her throne and motioned for Quinn to follow.

"Do you know why I summoned you?" she asked.

"No." Quinn fell into Imogen's shadow as they moved, striding toward the back of the throne room. The Queen walked with her head held high, a purposefulness to her steps as she reached for a half-concealed door and then pressed down on the gold-plated handle, easing the hatch open. She gestured for Quinn to go first.

Wary, Quinn walked, feeling as if she were on a plank and being doomed to the sea at a single word from the Queen, if Imogen so chose. It was disconcerting, and Quinn's fingers twitched, her power humming in her veins as she entered the darkened interior of the room. Behind her, Imogen chuckled, and the door closed, shutting them both in shadowed obscurity. Quinn closed her eyes, sensing Imogen's movements. There was no thrill of danger in the air, no ill intent, which both relieved and frustrated Quinn.

The soft motion of fabric being yanked sideways whooshed through the room as Imogen pulled on a dangling rope and moonlight—Leviathan's blessing—filtered into the space.

"This is my private chamber," the Queen said, lighting a candle and then another and another until the whole room was littered with small lights. "Feel free to take a seat."

Quinn eyed her from the side, watching as she flitted around the room, moving as though she were much younger than her appearance. Her attention quickly turned to the space when it seemed that Imogen was in no hurry to talk. A large four-poster bed. Gold engraving. A luxurious fur rug. Several chaise lounges, and overstuffed wing-backed chairs. The woman had a penchant for material luxuries. "I'm fine here," Quinn replied.

Imogen scoffed, but didn't say anything as she

strode for a long wooden bar at the back of the room and poured herself a healthy amount of amber liquid. She and Lazarus seemed to have an affinity in their taste of spirits. Quinn wrinkled her nose.

"I brought you here to ask you a few questions," Imogen said as she took her place upon a deep burgundy chaise lounge.

"I find it interesting I was granted an audience, but not my lord." Quinn lifted a brow. "Hoping that privacy means you can interrogate me?"

Imogen didn't answer her, but responded, none-theless. "How long have you known Lord Fierté?"

Quinn's mouth quirked. "Long enough."

"That's not an answer," the Queen pointed out.

"It's the only one you'll get from me."

Imogen sighed, tilting her glass up as half of the liquid in her cup disappeared in seconds.

Heavy drinker, then. Quinn mused. *Is she chasing away demons with those spirits? Or inviting them in?*

"This doesn't have to be difficult, Quinn. I am not an enemy."

"Then why won't you give him an audience?" Quinn asked, genuine curiosity pushing her to the question. *What could this woman possibly hope to gain by denying him a conversation?*

Imogen shook her head. "I haven't said I won't give him an audience—"

"And yet, here we are, almost a week later and you've still denied him an opportunity to speak with you." Perhaps it was not the wisest of actions to interrupt a Queen with a reputation like Imogen's, but Quinn had never been one to care.

It wasn't as if she were without power, both her own, and that of Neiss.

As if sensing her change in thoughts, the ancient serpent peeked its eye open, watching the situation from Quinn's eyes. Listening to the things she left unsaid.

Imogen lifted a brow as she downed the rest of her drink. "Sit," she commanded.

Quinn held for a moment, debating the consequences of disobeying such an order—but decided it wasn't worth the repercussions. She sat on the edge of a royal blue, wing-backed chair and waited as Imogen refilled her glass before striding back to her lounge and reclining once more. She sipped delicately this time, taking care with the liquid as she hadn't the first glass. *Perhaps she is drowning her own demons if she drinks this heavily.* Quinn was cataloguing each and every movement to decipher later.

"Do you know the difficulties of ruling a kingdom, Quinn?" Imogen didn't wait for an answer. "The burden of being a dignitary is that everyone is looking to find a way to use you, fuck you, or kill you—so they can take your place." She licked the amber spirits from her lips. "I'm sure your lord has some knowledge of that."

Quinn stiffened.

"As Queen, I must know just as much about my friends as I do about my enemies, perhaps more." Her eyes appeared cloudy, and a weariness had entered her expression.

"Which is Lazarus?" Quinn asked.

Imogen's lips curved upward as her dark eyes met Quinn's stare. "That has yet to be determined." Shifting so that one leg crossed the other, Imogen leaned forward. "You are interesting to me, Quinn. That's why I asked you here. Lord Fierté has become quite well-known as the heir to end the reign of blood in Norcasta. He is infamous for the shadowed whispers that follow him everywhere he goes." Imogen leaned back again with a huff of irritation. "Unfortunately, however, most of what I've heard are just that—whispers, rumors. None of it can be proven."

"What is it that you want to prove?"

Imogen set her empty glass down on a stone-carved table at her side and crossed her legs again. "I want to know what kind of man he is."

Quinn frowned, her eyes tracking the Queen's movements as she shifted, the darker woman's hands sliding to the side as she gripped the arms of her chair and met Quinn's watchful gaze. "That still doesn't explain why you brought me here," Quinn said. "What kind of man he is isn't exactly something I can speak to."

"I beg to differ." Imogen gave her a sly smile.

"I didn't know Queens begged for anything," she replied.

Imogen barked out a surprised laugh as she leaned to one side, wiping her eyes as they filled with tears of mirth. "You do so amuse me, Quinn of House Fierté. Alas, you are not wrong. There is very little I would ever feel the desire to beg for."

"I doubt anyone ever truly feels the *desire* to beg," Quinn replied. "If they do beg, it's likely out of need."

Imogen hummed; a non-response that was reply enough. The Pirate Queen dropped her hands, but not her guard. Her face was as imperceptible as it was beautifully unique. "Perhaps you're right," she finally said, "but that's not why I called you here."

"Yes," Quinn said. "You wanted to know more

about Lazarus. Why you called me here to answer your questions—regardless of your interest in me—still makes no sense. There is little about Lazarus that I know that you likely don't."

Imogen shook her head and settled her gaze on Quinn with an eerie focus that made Quinn's own attention sharpen. "Why do you think his character is not something that you can speak to?" Imogen asked.

"I think you misunderstand." Quinn kept her eyes locked with Imogen's. The whole of the conversation felt like a farce to Quinn; a test. "Whatever whispers you've heard are likely all there is to know about him. I have no extra information to provide. Should you desire more, I suggest you ask him directly."

Imogen's lips twitched into a smirk. "Fair enough," she replied with a nod. "But I still believe there are some things where your opinion on the matter would hold . . . weight."

"Such as?"

"His capacity for loyalty," she finally answered.

Quinn frowned. "You're asking me if I think he's loyal?"

Imogen didn't respond, but merely waited on

Quinn expectantly. Silence echoed in the private chamber.

"I don't know what you want me to say," Quinn spoke with a sharpness of tongue, her patience finally running thin. "You bring me here to question me, but you dance with your words. Speak plainly. I'm not a diplomat. What is it you're really after, Imogen? Are you a Queen of Pirates or a Queen of Evasion?"

Imogen doubled over and released a torrent of laughter, peals of it coming from between her lips so suddenly that it appeared as though she had succumbed to some sort of hysteria. A madness. "Queen of Evasion," she finally said, calming after several moments. Still, her body seemed to shake even as she composed herself once more. "Now, that's an accusation I haven't heard before. It's a wonder no one's thought of it."

Quinn silently fumed as she stared at the other woman. She knew it was not wise to oppose or rebuke a woman with such power, but Quinn felt that buzzing still. The drive of her power—and it wasn't coming from her. *Is the Queen afraid of something?*

"I want to know if I can trust Lord Fierté," Imogen admitted, boring her intense stare into

Quinn. "I want to know if Lazarus will be the end of my kingdom or if he'll be a help to my reign. I want to know, through his own vassals, what kind of man your Lord is. I brought you here because you seem quite candid. So, can you, a N'skari woman, under the thumb of a Norcastan noble, tell me if I should trust the man or not?"

Quinn shook her head. "I'm afraid," she said slowly, "that you'll have to find out the answers for yourself."

The Queen tilted her head to the side but didn't appear to be upset or enraged as Quinn predicted. "You're unexpected. Quite unexpected."

Quinn's back stiffened. "What does that mean?"

When Imogen turned her head, bringing her arm up to rest on the arm of her chaise, Quinn noted a bead of sweat slide from beneath the woman's hairline down her jaw. "The N'skari are known for keeping to themselves. They rarely, if ever, allow outsiders into their midst. And just as well, they also rarely leave their country. The coldness of N'skara is unnatural—it keeps more than the people away; it keeps those born within it sequestered against the rest of the world. I can count on one hand how many N'skari I've met in my lifetime. You may look N'skari, and whether you were at one point in your life—on the inside—you no longer are."

Quinn's expression closed off as if shutters were falling over her eyes—hiding her thoughts away from the perceptive Queen. N'skara might have been her homeland, but even as a child, she'd never fit in. Quinn was a black Maji in a sea of light Maji that looked down upon the gray. Black was a stain in their society. A sin. She had been a secret and a weapon. It seemed the more things changed in this world, the more they stayed the same . . . but not her. Not Quinn. As a child, that darkness lurked, and as a young woman, it festered and rotted. It grew. She may look like the people she longed to return to . . . but only the wicked understood how evil hid in plain sight.

She and her people were the same in that—and only that.

Imogen rested her head on her palm, sighing heavily. She blinked slowly, her eyelids sliding closed for a moment longer each time until she forced her eyes open with a jerk and dropped her arm, standing from her seat.

"Can I trust him?" she demanded.

"Can you ever truly trust anyone without reservation?" Quinn replied. Imogen glanced back at her and smiled.

"You say you're not a diplomat, but you speak the pretty words as well as I do," the Queen said.

"I speak honest ones," Quinn replied. "He wants an alliance. You know this, but you ask yourself if you can trust him completely. I don't understand why it's even a question. Alliances exist to benefit you both; not to be friends. This is an exchange made for power."

Imogen watched her shrewdly. "Very well. Tell me—is he a kind master?" Another bead of sweat slid down her face. "Is he cruel? Does he pay you well? How much?"

Quinn pursed her lips and didn't respond.

Imogen chuckled, a raspy noise in her throat. She coughed as the amusement subsided—a wet hacking sound. Quinn frowned, but before she could say anything, Imogen went on. "What would you say if I told you that I could offer you ten times as much as he pays you?" she said. "I'll make the offer, you know. You interest me, Quinn, and I think my daughter admires you."

Imogen took a step forward, stumbling a bit as her hand shot out and steadied her against one of the stone tables. "What say you?" she asked again, panting.

Quinn moved forward; her hand outstretched. "Are you—"

"I'm fine." The Queen waved her off before standing upright again. "Answer the question. Would you consider joining Ilvas?"

Stubborn as she was, she was obviously exhausted. The signs were as clear as the dark circles forming under her eyes. Still, she stood tall, her gaze dark and fiery, albeit clouded over with an obscure haze.

Quinn shook her head. "You couldn't offer me enough money in the world," she said. "What Lazarus provides—what he will provide me with if he wants to continue to use my power—is far more valuable than all of the glittering jewels in your kingdom."

Imogen laughed, and the sound hurt Quinn's ears. Curling her lips in confusion and disgust, Quinn took a step back as Imogen's laughter turned into yet another hacking cough. A knock on the door distracted her for a moment, but in the next instance, a wet, bubbly noise recaptured her attention.

"What—"

With the Queen's next cough, a splattering of blood erupted from her lips. Red droplets hit the marbled floors, crimson stained the fur rug, and a single bead ran from the top of Quinn's boots.

Imogen panted as she doubled over, one hand pressed to her abdomen. She cursed in Ilvan as the door opened and the top of Zorel's head appeared. "My Queen?"

Dark eyes encased in true fear raised to meet Quinn's gaze, sending a sizzle of addictive power sliding through her veins. Zorel's eyes widened as he took in the scene—Imogen reaching up for Quinn with drawn brows and blood dribbling from the corner of her mouth.

"I've been poisoned," Imogen half-whispered, half-coughed as she fell against Quinn's front.

Her arms went out to catch the fallen woman and blood smeared her ivory skin, creating streaks of red down her arms.

"Guards!" Zorel shouted.

Quinn jerked her head up as the doors were flung even wider and several armed men intruded. Zorel glared at Quinn—his ominous gaze drilling into her as he pointed. "Arrest her on the grounds of treason. She's poisoned the Queen."

War and Reason

"Some creatures are simply too powerful to be strong-armed into compliance. Where fear cannot motivate, reason can."
— Lazarus Fierté, soul eater, heir to Norcasta, cunning prince

Lazarus paced restlessly through the chamber. His half decanter of spirits left forgotten on the tableside as the fire roared in the hearth, courtesy of the firedrakes temper beneath his skin. The creatures within him were growing bolder in Quinn's absence. Where before the removal of the basilisk would have made them easier to handle, in truth, they had only become more difficult. With his emotions fraying dangerously close to madness and the beasts continued relentlessness, Lazarus felt the edge drawing near.

He clenched his fist, and the flames died down as the firedrake sensed its master's ire was not far. The beast, unable to act on its baser instinct, scratched and clawed at his insides for a moment before settling with a huff of its lethal feathers.

"I'm sure it will be alright, Lazarus," Draeven started, pulling him from his reverie. "Quinn's a bit brash but, then, Imogen was a pirate. They're probably swapping stories about people they've ransacked or killed by this point . . ." His left-hand's eyebrows drew together for a moment, his lips pinching. "On second thought, perhaps worrying isn't the worst thing."

Lazarus scowled. It was bad enough the Queen had sent her child as the envoy, and not a dignitary —but she still refused him an audience and instead granted it to Quinn. He thought this was all part of her games, and that she'd question Quinn and decide from that. He couldn't shake the thought that perhaps there was more to it.

His eyes narrowed on the door as an unbidden thought crept into his mind that was all his own. *If she's taken an audience with Quinn to try to lure her away from me, it will be at the expense of her kingdom.* Lazarus' fists squeezed, his knuckles turning white as he considered all the ways Imogen might try to convince Quinn to change sides.

"Lazarus," Draeven said warily. He sat up in the lounge, setting his grapes aside. His movements were slow, exaggerated with a purpose. "What has your souls vying for power? What are you thinking?" His violet eyes dropped to Lazarus' wrists, where inky shadows had indeed started to inch their way around his cuffs.

"Imogen is a smart woman and a vicious Queen. She granted an audience for Quinn alone, and I can't help but wonder if there might be more to it." Lazarus turned away from his friend and toward the fire as he inhaled slow, even breaths, pushing the souls down, back into submission.

"You don't think—"

"I do," Lazarus said. "Quinn is invaluable. Priceless. With her, Imogen doesn't need to align with anyone to keep her kingdom out of war. The entire Sirian continent could fall and she'd be able to withstand."

Draeven shook his head and sighed. "Quinn wouldn't change sides, Laz, no matter what Imogen offered."

"What makes you say that?"

Draeven continued, coming to stand beside him. "Weren't you listening to a word of what she said before she left? Quinn doesn't value gold or jewels. She values power—and freedom." Lazarus considered this for a moment.

"And you don't think that Imogen could offer her those?"

"Assuming she could even find a way around the contract, which as far as you or I know is impossible —no, I don't think she could." Lazarus shook his head, still unsure, and not liking it. When had the tables turned so much, Lazarus was no longer certain who was the master. Since when had Draeven begun to speak of her loyalty, when only a month ago he had been so certain she was a bad idea?

"What makes you so certain Quinn would stay?" Lazarus asked quietly.

Draeven stared into the flames, the red glint reflecting on his face as the fire danced between light and shadow. "Answer me this. If Quinn came to you today about her enemies—would you stop her from seeking vengeance?"

Lazarus rubbed his forehead. *Would I stop her from seeking vengeance?* Understanding clicked within him. He turned away, and though he didn't answer aloud, Lazarus knew the truth. No, he wouldn't stop her. He didn't have any desire to stop her. Instead, Lazarus craved to guide her into being the weapon she was meant to be. He wanted to wield her as one might a sword. Only in the past week had he seen the repercussions from his actions. To control a powerhouse like Quinn was to risk one's own safety, but if the reins were too tight, he would risk her turning on him. His true concern. Because while Quinn clung to the darkness inside her like a soldier did their sword, if he wanted to continue to be the beholder of that power, he had to accept there would be slips. Accidental and not.

Imogen wouldn't allow her the same graces, and for that, she would never take her.

Lazarus' fist unclenched, and Draeven sighed in relief.

"You need to fuck her and get it over with," his left-hand said, turning again for his lounge. Lazarus tensed all over again, but before he could reply, a thundering of footsteps in the hall caught his attention.

What in the dark realm . . .

The door flew open, banging against the stonewall behind it as guards in blue and white flooded into the room with their weapons drawn. They encircled him and Draeven, swords raised, the metal blades glinting in the firelight. Lazarus was only briefly aware of other doors being thrown open as more guards charged in. A nameless voice yelled in Ilvan from within one of the rooms.

There were several umphs followed by a groan before Vaughn was dragged from the suite he'd retreated to in Quinn's absence. The soldiers shoved him into the circle, and the Cisean warrior garnered a tiny bit more respect from Lazarus as he jumped to his feet and bared his teeth, letting out a roar of outrage. Vaughn banged his chest with one closed fist, spit flying from his mouth. The soldier in front of him took a step back, his sword wavering a fraction as the unarmed mountain man showed his true colors. While he might be a dog, and a well-trained one around Quinn, dogs were still beasts when cornered all the same.

Too many voices were speaking for Lazarus to get a clear idea of who or what was being said. The creatures inside him vied to be let out. To defend their master. To slaughter those that tried to kill their keeper. Like Vaughn, they were beasts—and while they might not have bodies anymore, the instincts were still there.

"Pity," came a reply in Norcastan. Lazarus narrowed his gaze as two Ilvan men briefly parted to allow through none other than the Queen's advisor, Zorel. "Search the grounds for the weapons master. The Queen's in danger so long as House Fierté remains unguarded."

"What are you talking about?" Lazarus demanded, war and reason clashing within him. A sense of dread settled in his stomach as he thought of Quinn's meeting with the Queen . . .

What has she done?

"Lazarus Fierté, you are under house arrest and will remain in your quarters by order of the crown," Zorel stated with a lazy smirk. Lazarus' blood boiled as contention within him began to win over his more reasonable side.

"I am a nobleman and heir to Norcasta—by law, you are required to justify your actions," he replied in a voice that spoke of impending bloodshed, should his wishes not be heeded.

"Lord Fierté, I don't know what false impressions you are under, but Ilvas is Imogen's realm, and given that the Queen is currently indisposed—the only law we are required to follow currently is by *my* word."

Lazarus' eyes flashed, and the flames in the

hearth roared, blowing out of the fireplace only inches from the guards that surrounded them. Several cries of dismay sounded as the three closest to him leapt back, only just beginning to understand the power they were attempting to control.

Zorel's expression hardened. "I would reconsider before attempting something like that again if you wish to walk out of here with your head still attached to your shoulders, Lord Fierté."

"I would reconsider threatening me if *you or your men* have any desire to make it out of this room as more than ashes," Lazarus replied with a coldness that seemed to spread through the air despite the fire's barely contained flames. A sliver of something broke through the smug mask the advisor wore. If Quinn were here, she'd have made him eat his spleen for such words.

Gods, Lazarus needed to find her and figure out what had happened.

Zorel's mask fell back into place as he frowned and peered over with a look of distaste. He tsked once, and Lazarus ground his teeth in an effort to restrain himself. He needed information from the man before he killed him.

Draeven stepped up, not quite blocking them from each other, but clearly intending to distract

Lazarus with his presence. "It would be much easier for us to comply with your terms if we had an idea of why you're putting us under house arrest, and why the Queen couldn't give these orders herself?" Draeven prompted. He was calm, his hands unshaking, his eyes serene as he spoke diplomatically. The man was Lazarus' left-hand for a reason. His demeanor made him as well suited for it as Quinn's cruelty made her to be his right.

"Very well. If it will make you *comply*." He paused, emphasizing the word in Lazarus' direction. As if this were an actual trade. *Foolish skeev*. "The Queen has been poisoned, and your assassin is to blame."

Lazarus felt a rage of heat overtake him for a brief moment as the words hit him, and then came the bitter sting of ice as he let them sink in.

Poisoned. Imogen had been poisoned.

With that one piece of information, Lazarus learned three things that Zorel likely hadn't meant to reveal.

First, Quinn most definitely had not killed her.

Secondly, she was obviously being framed for someone else's actions and therefore she was in danger—and when Quinn was in danger, that meant *all of them* were in danger. These halfwits had no idea the beast they had provoked.

The third and final piece of information was that Imogen's court had a traitor. One close enough to poison her, and smart enough to frame Lazarus' house for it.

He set a hard gaze on Zorel as the thoughts began whirling. He didn't make his move known here. Lazarus was smarter than that. With a heavy sigh, he stepped back and leaned against the wall beside the window.

"I don't have an assassin in my employment, of that I can assure you. If you need to launch an investigation while we remain here, be my guest." Lazarus smiled, pulling a card from Quinn's book. Even Draeven frowned at the change of heart, none of them the wiser to the creature he'd called forth from beneath his skin and sent to find the one member of his house that was still free.

Dominicus needed to stay gone and start hunting.

Dungeon of Deception

"If it looks like a rat and talks like a rat—it's a rat."
— *Quinn Darkova, vassal of House Fierté, fear twister,*
mistaken assassin

Q uinn paced the confines of the cell, tilting her head and cracking her neck as she silently fumed. She had only been with Imogen for a short while. *How had she been poisoned in that time?* Quinn stopped in front of the stone wall of her prison and growled as she punched again. Her knuckles were already bruised, the skin scraped raw, but that was only a slight pain compared to the panic slowly setting in at being caged. She had to keep her wits, and her temper, about her if she wanted to make it out of here alive.

What would Lazarus do? she wondered. *What would he think?* Dust rained down on her, and Quinn shook her head, flinging it away from her hair as she turned and continued her pacing.

It didn't matter what Lazarus would do or think, Quinn decided. She wasn't even sure if they would inform him of her arrest or not. If they did, then he should understand that she let herself be arrested. Her innocence—at least in this—was evident.

What mattered now was what *she* was going to do.

"Perhaps I could be of assistance?" Neiss said, coming forth from her inner mind.

Quinn stumbled a bit at the feeling of his body—a tattoo on her skin—as he moved from her back to her front, sliding around under her flesh. Quinn shivered. It wasn't painful, but it was unsettling.

"What are you offering?" Quinn asked aloud.

Quinn stared down at the skin of her forearm as Neiss' head slithered forth and solidified, growing heavier as he detached himself from her and dropped down to the ground. Neiss hissed at the coldness of the stone and coiled tight, lifting his head.

"*I offer my senses,*" he said. "*My eyes.*" The end of his dark mauve tail flicked back and forth. "*While you remain here, I do not have to.*"

Quinn considered this. "You could go see the Queen," she stated. "And inform Lazarus of what's happened, if he hasn't already been told?" Neiss nodded, his slender, arrow-shaped skull bobbing with the movement.

"*I can show you.*"

"Show me?" Quinn asked.

Neiss' dark black tongue flicked out, tasting the air before he rose up, his head expanding as his dark, sable eyes bore into hers. It was like staring straight into the abyss . . . until a fuzzy image began to form in her mind. One of her, as she was in that moment, in her blood-stained tunic and frazzled hair. The image was distorted, the colors too muted and the angles too sharp. Her face was white— paler than she'd ever seen it. Her hair a darkened gray. The blood on her skin appeared black. There were no colors in the ashen lens the snake looked upon the world with.

"*You can see as I see, master,*" Neiss said. "*We are one soul, you and I.*"

"Yet, you call me master."

The creature tilted its head, almost like it was thoughtful. *"What do you wish to be called, young one?"*

"Quinn will suffice. I desire to be no one's master, Neiss, not even yours," she said.

"So be it."

Neiss began to shrink in size, making himself no longer than her forearm. Quinn clenched her jaw, not liking how vulnerable he appeared to be. "You say we share a soul . . . what happens if you die, Neiss?"

The tiny creature slithered over her boot, and she knew it to be an affectionate gesture through the slight hum of contentment that ran through her.

"I am but a sliver in your soul. If I were to die, you would remain, Quinn." That ancient voice spoke with such assuredness and without fear that she wasn't sure what to think. It was strange to have another being inside oneself; one that did not feel fear such as she did.

"And if I die?" she asked quietly.

"We shall both perish."

Quinn wasn't sure what to think of that answer, nor the feeling that settled in her chest as she said, "You realize that if you get caught, it's not likely I'll be able to save you. This world holds no love for snakes."

"I will not be captured," Neiss assured her.

"How do you know?" she asked. "Have you done this before? For Lazarus?"

The snake watched her, almost thoughtful in its reptilian stare. *"Before you, I was his to command; and before him, I was another's. All my life, I've been used for my eyes. A vessel to further other's plans."*

"I don't want to use you," she said, her lips pressing together. "Not if it will endanger you. I value our bond more than that."

"I will not be captured," Neiss repeated. *"This I know."*

Quinn crossed her arms over her chest, and she sighed. "I don't want you doing this, but I also don't see another option—not while I'm trapped in here and whoever poisoned the Queen is running around doing Gods' knows what." He slithered over her boot and brushed against her as if he were a cat. Quinn waved her arm to the four stone walls that surrounded her.

She wasn't completely certain, but she suspected there had to be a way out of here. The tiny window fifteen-feet above the ground wasn't an option and the iron bars held where there was not stone, but

Quinn had been in—and gotten out of—worse predicaments before. The question was, should she? Quinn hadn't poisoned the Queen, but if she ran, they would surely think she did. Still, the real would-be killer was free while she was not, and someone had to find them. If she tried to escape and failed to find the right person and proof before she was caught, though . . .

Quinn stopped and glanced out the tiny window at Leviathan's eye. Already hours had passed, and there had been no word from anyone besides the ones she heard filtering down the hall outside her cell on occasion. The guards here liked to talk and were often loud given they had no idea she could understand them. Not that they'd revealed any real information beyond the hope that Imogen would want to punish her if she woke. They were very much looking forward to the possible chance to use Quinn's body if the Queen chose that form of torture before death. There was only one man she'd consider taking with her body, and any others would find themselves with a shattered mind and slit throat before they could attempt it. Still . . . their talks put her on edge. She wouldn't be in this position had she not been framed. "When I find whoever did this, I'll be sure to make them suffer." Black tendrils leaked from her fingertips. She couldn't help how her rage affected the fear beneath her skin. "I have a feeling the culprit is much closer than even Imogen knows."

"Would you have me search them out?" Neiss asked.

Quinn shook her head, tossing a glance back at the large oak door on the other side of the dungeon. "No. I want you to go check on the Queen. Inform me of her condition. If she dies, then my timeline moves up."

"Timeline?"

"Yes, I'll need to decide if I want to bide my time in here"—she cast a look around. She'd lived through far worse circumstances—"or if I want to escape."

"If the Queen lives?"

Quinn turned back to face the snake. "Then find Lazarus." In her mind, she added, *"Be safe, Neiss. I'll tell you what to do when you reach him."*

Neiss slithered through the bars of the cell and over the compact dirt. Footsteps sounded in the hallway beyond, making Quinn freeze, though Neiss continued moving, barely visible to even her eye. She whirled around, facing the opposite direction as a key jingled on the other side and the door swung inward, those footsteps coming to a stop outside her prison.

She glanced at the floor despite Zorel's presence, but Neiss had already slipped through and was gone. Quinn lifted her gaze to Imogen's advisor's. She stepped forward until she was within an arm's reach of the cell bars. The man watched her with displeasure, and she raised a brow when he stepped forward as well, a small curve forming to the corner of his mouth.

"Enjoying your new accommodations?" he asked, his tone thick with self-satisfaction.

Quinn tilted her head. "I did not poison your Queen," she said. "But then, you already knew that, didn't you?" Zorel scowled. Yes, she'd been right. The true assassin was much closer to the Queen than Imogen had realized. He had to have poisoned the alcohol. That was the only thing she'd drank while with Quinn.

"Careful there. That sounds awfully close to an accusation," he replied. The corners of his eyes wrinkled, and his lips tightened.

"Maybe it is," she said, unable to stop the words. "Maybe I happen to know this is all a farce." She motioned to him, and the advisor narrowed his eyes.

"I came to interrogate the would-be assassin who poisoned our Queen," he replied tartly, folding his arms across his chest.

"You mean you came to gloat about overthrowing a crown you won't be able to hold," Quinn answered in kind. "I believe that's what you meant to say."

"One might think you'd be a bit more respectful when the penalty for trying to kill the Queen is death," he said, trying to throw her.

"Yes, one might think," she agreed. "I wonder how Imogen will take it when she's learned one of her closest advisors pulled this." Quinn leaned inward, raising her hands to the bars. She wrapped her chilled fingers around the iron rods. The metal was almost warm beneath her grip. "She doesn't strike me as the forgiving type."

Zorel frowned to mask his expression, but she didn't miss the way he unfolded his arms to tug at his sleeves. When she let the silence span, he began to pace, shooting her distrustful glances every few moments. The golden slippers on his feet padded heavily against the compact dirt floors, not that Zorel seemed to care or mind. He probably had a thousand gold slippers and need not worry about dirtying them with his heavy footfalls, even though a single shoe could probably buy ten slaves. Quinn grimaced as she watched him turnabout, and the fine robe which he wore swished back and forth.

"You should do yourself a favor," she said. "Confess. I promise to make it quick. You won't feel Imogen's wrath, which is considerably kinder than my own should you not." Her tone darkened, and Zorel swallowed.

"You mean to threaten me?"

"Yes," she said simply. "Because no matter what Imogen can do to you, I will be ten times worse." His face paled, and the tiny black eyes seemed to bulge out of his head as a vein in his temple throbbed.

"This is treason. You'll hang for this," he insisted.

Quinn scoffed. "We both know I didn't try to kill her. I don't poison when I kill, and Lazarus will know that. Poison is for cowards." She gave him a pointed lift of her brows that made his cheeks flush red with anger while he simultaneously stiffened.

My, my, do I dare hope you already played that card to my *master? I think I do.*

"Deny it all you want," Zorel snapped, "but it will not save you from the noose."

"I'm not afraid of the noose, Zorel." Quinn

took a step closer, her shoulders pressing into the bars as her hands curled around the cold metal. "Are you?"

He straightened his shoulders and met Quinn's eyes with a semi-confident stare. "Where did you get the poison?"

"You said would-be," Quinn said instead. "That means, she's still alive, right?"

"For now." He looked her over, and she sensed his fear.

"Is that a threat?" she asked. "Do you mean to go back and finish the job?"

"These accusations are baseless—"

"I am innocent, at least of this, and there is no other person in this court that has ties to Norcasta. Do you know what's going on in Norcasta right now?" He swallowed, and Quinn smiled. "So you do. Which means you know of the heirs, and if you somehow turn out to be connected to them . . ." She let the words trail, making her thoughts clear.

Zorel swallowed again, his skin glistening in the sliver of moonlight. Beads of sweat dotted his temple as he cleared his throat. "Whether you confess or not, you will be tried and hanged for what you have done," he said slowly. His voice was sure, but not confident. Steady, but not sound.

"Answer me this," Quinn said, pressing her face against the bars. "Why would someone who's been summoned by the Queen be left alone with her?" When Zorel didn't reply, Quinn pressed forward. "Isn't she constantly guarded for situations just like this?"

"She requested privacy for your audience with her," Zorel said immediately, as if that answered anything.

"Why would a would-be assassin not cover their tracks, hmmm? Why would I be the one found alone with her if I were the one to make an attempt on her life?"

"Y-you were caught in the act," he stuttered. "Don't stand there and deny your involvement—"

"Confess or I will find a way out of this cell and hunt you down myself," Quinn said quietly. "I don't know why you did it exactly, but I plan to find out."

Zorel stumbled back, the force of his fear rising. "Y-you will not get away with this."

"Neither will you."

She could sense his fear. The more she talked, the headier the scent. It wafted from him, filtering through the space between them. He reeked of sweat, guilt, and anxiety. It made Quinn's mouth water and the buzz of her power strengthen. Had she wanted to, she could have ripped the proverbial floor out from beneath Zorel and sent him careening into a nightmare of his own making while she easily slipped out into the night, unscathed and liberated from her unjust arrest.

But the Queen was alive. Attacking him now would only aid his accusations and not her own.

He shook his head and stumbled back to the door, scrambling to get the latch undone. Quinn sighed and backed away from the bars. *Nothing but a spineless animal*, she thought. *Looking for weakness where there is none.*

The sound of Zorel slamming the door behind him echoed into the night as Quinn's vision faltered under the weight of the first image Neiss was sending her. A blurry shock of black and white—a lavish bed and a sleeping Queen. She was alive, but the pallor of her skin and trembles in her form gave Quinn pause. She'd seen those signs before.

Just as the blood in her veins turned to ice and a cold fury descended on her, Quinn heard something. A soft thump of boots against the dirt floor.

Someone was in her cell.

Tenuous Allies

"Power might corrupt, but naivety kills."
— *Quinn Darkova, vassal of House Fierté, fear twister,*
framed assassin

T he sharp edge of a blade pressed against Quinn's throat.

She blinked, jerking away, and the image faded. Replacing the opulent chaise and bright pillows were grime-smeared walls and a plume of dust that made her gag as her instincts rammed into her. A slight sting started toward the tip of the blade, spreading across as the edge was slowly dragged over the soft flesh of her throat. Unable to feel fear but understanding the need to protect herself all the same, she drew on her magic. Black wisps floated off her skin, and the person holding the knife faltered. The grip was strong, but the assailant small as she noticed a pale hand smaller than her own that shook before her face.

"What in the ever-lovin' fish fuc—" The knife slipped from the girl's grip and landed with a loud clatter against the dirt floor. Quinn brought her elbow back and landed a blow against the person at her back, connecting with soft skin rather than hard bone. She whirled around and brought her forearm up, pressing it into the girl's throat as she backed her against the opposite stone wall of her prison cell.

"If your goal was to irritate me," Quinn stated blandly as she glared down at Axe's upturned face while the girl struggled to breathe against the pressure on her throat, "you've succeeded."

Axe squirmed against Quinn's immovable grip. "Release me," she choked out.

One violet brow lifted as Quinn said, "Explain why you were attempting to sneak up on me with a dagger in hand and I *might*," she pressed her arm in harder, "let you go."

Axe narrowed her eyes, lips pushing together as

she leveled Quinn with a look of suspicion. "My *madara* was the one poisoned. I think *I'll* be askin' the questions."

"Hmm," Quinn mused. "Considering I'm not the one with her back against the wall, I think we can safely say you're no longer calling the shots where I'm concerned, Urchin," Quinn said mockingly.

Axe's brow furrowed as she glowered at Quinn. Her lips smashed together in an exaggerated frown before she got the terrible idea to attempt surging forward. If Quinn wasn't already expecting the outburst, the girl might have actually wrangled herself free. As it was, Quinn pressed even harder, and Axe choked, coming up short. Her lips parted as her blue eyes watered—from emotion or lack of air, Quinn didn't know.

"Only family"—she coughed once, and Quinn lessened her hold—"calls me that, *hussy.*"

"And where's your family right now while that weasel throws whomever he likes in prison and your mother lays dying?" Quinn asked. The girl's bottom lip trembled, but Axe bit down on it, her eyes flashing with ire.

"Don't know. Tellin' me wasn't exactly anyone's first priority."

Quinn sighed and abruptly stepped away, dropping her arm. Axe stumbled for a moment before reaching for one of the axes at her hip. Quinn twisted her fingers and black tendrils shot from them, curling around the child's wrist.

Axe stilled.

"I wouldn't do that if I were you," Quinn warned. The tendrils slithered back, releasing her, but the girl was smart and didn't reach for her weapon again. Instead, she crossed her arms over her chest and tapped her foot.

"Did you poison her?" she demanded. "I need to hear you say it."

Quinn looked her straight in the eye and said, "No, I did not poison your Queen. As I told Zorel, if I was going to kill someone"—Quinn lifted one finger—"one—I wouldn't poison them," she said as she lifted a second. "And two—I wouldn't be dumb enough to be caught at the scene of the crime."

Some of the tension drained out of Axe, but the expression on her face was that of a scared child playing at being strong. Her eyes held a glassy sheen, making the blue brighter and accentuating the redness from crying. She sniffled once, wiping her nose with the back of her hand and then glancing away to hide it. Dark emotions circled in her chest, eating at her from the inside out. Her frazzled red hair and nervous movements were the only outward signs of how distressed she was at the possibility of losing the only mother she'd ever known.

Quinn didn't understand it.

Then again, she didn't understand most people's love of family.

"Is there a chance that Lord Fierté might have done it?" Axe asked softly. She didn't sound as if she considered Lazarus' involvement to be possible, but she also didn't seem to have another place to start.

"Why would he poison her? He hasn't even been granted an audience yet," Quinn said. "Not that I think he's going to get one now." Quinn sighed, pushing that aside as another problem for another day. One where her life wasn't on the line. Then again, those days seemed to be fewer and fewer the longer she was in Lazarus' company. While she didn't go hungry and had money in her coin purse, the reality of being a vassal to an heir such as him was that they were always in danger. Where there was power, there were hands to reach for it.

"Maybe he only wanted an audience to get

close to her, and you were the next best thing." Axe shrugged.

Quinn rolled her eyes. "If Lazarus wanted Imogen dead, she would be. He would not risk her recovery on a poison that may or may not work when there are more effective methods that would guarantee . . ." she paused, her gaze sweeping over Axe. "Removal from this world."

"Such as?"

"Me," Quinn said flatly. "I could drive her out of her mind with fear. Make her put a knife through her heart." She trailed her fingers over her own chest, pointing to the spot beneath her breast. "Or I could make her guards kill her. Less suspicious that way and no one would ever know." Her hand dropped back to her side, and Quinn shrugged. "Or, even still, I could stab her myself and disappear into the night before anyone was the wiser."

"Have you done that?" Axe asked. "Killed people before?"

Quinn turned, a dark grin on her lips. "No, but I've made people wish I did. Death is kinder than what I choose to do."

Axe frowned, eyeing her warily. "Is that what you're goin' to do to me?"

"Depends," Quinn said, her gaze sweeping over

the cell. Axe had dropped from the window fifteen feet above, evidence of the dirt on her hands and forearms. Flecks splattered her skin like freckles. "You came here because you thought my lord and I wanted your mother dead. What do you plan to do now that you know it wasn't us?"

"I don't know for certain it wasn't—"

"Would you like me to detail more ways I could kill her and not be caught, because I could come up with a dozen off the top of my head that wouldn't have ended with me in this cell."

"Ugh," Axe groaned in frustration. "You've made your point. If you wanted her dead, she would be. But if it's not you, then who?"

"Zorel."

"What?" She blinked, frowning at the ground. "That makes no sense. I mean, don't get me wrong —he's a weasel-faced git, but that doesn't mean he tried to poison *Madara*."

"Tell me this," Quinn said. "Who declared me the poisoner? Who was the first in the room? Who hasn't told you anything? Who is in charge while she's unconscious and barely clinging to life?"

"How do you know about—"

"I have my ways," Quinn answered dismissively. "As I'm sure your mother's advisor does."

Axe's lips pinched together as she turned in circles, glaring at the ground while she mulled over the probability. The howl of the wind over the water outside Tritol dulled the quieter things: the rustle of animals in the night, the caw of sandgulls as they dove for their prey, the whispers surrounding Imogen's poisoning. The guards in the hall laughed jovially about something Quinn couldn't quite hear, seeming lost in the same drunken stupor as the rest of the city despite recent events.

"How do I know you're not just placin' blame on him to distract me?" Axe asked.

"You don't," Quinn answered. "But consider this, Lazarus has enough going on with trying to secure Norcasta to even consider something like dethroning the Queen. Aren't there measures in place for who would rule in Imogen's absence anyway?" Quinn asked.

Axe nodded. "I would."

Quinn paused. The idea of letting a mere teen girl lead something as immense as a nation seemed incredibly stupid to her, but she didn't say as much. Instead, she shook her head and proceeded. "Then even if he were to kill your mother, it still doesn't leave a throne open for him to take. I have a feeling that people like your Aunt Petra would be a problem. With the situation regarding the blood heirs . . ." Quinn trailed. "Lazarus can't fight two wars at once right now. Imogen knows that. Zorel knows that. Now you know that. It's why we're here. He needs allies to fight even one." There was a fine line between explaining enough to get them out of scrutiny and betraying his trust, and Quinn had no desire to walk that line, even if she was already on death row.

Lazarus had a way of making even the dead pay.

"He might not have a motivation, but neither does Zorel," Axe argued.

"He's an advisor that hails from Norcasta. The Queen was attacked during my audience, while I was trying to gain one for my lord—a man who will be the next king of Norcasta and is fighting his own private war with the blood heirs." Quinn leaned back against the wall, crossing one ankle over the other while she cocked her head.

"Do you really think—"

"I do," Quinn said. "It doesn't require being a truth siever to see that he's the most questionable one in this court with the greatest possible ties to Norcasta, and the timing is too convenient to be anything but an elaborate setup."

Axe peered at her almost thoughtfully in her expression before she shook her head. "But you can't prove it, can you?"

Quinn exhaled heavily. "In here? No more than anyone else can prove I did it. Out there"—she jutted her chin toward the door on the other side of the barred-iron wall—"I'd have to track him down, but I could do it."

"You're sure?" Axe asked.

"I wouldn't say I could if I wasn't," Quinn replied.

Axe sighed, uncrossing her arms to hook her thumbs in her pockets. "I think you're probably a murderer and maybe even a liar, but not in this."

"What makes you say that?" Quinn asked curiously.

Axe smiled. "*Madara* taught me many things. How to spot a liar was one."

Quinn wasn't sure if she should be offended or relieved. "I could be an exceptionally good liar," she countered.

Axe sucked a tooth obnoxiously and said, "Are you tryin' to convince me or not?" Quinn shrugged.

"I don't think it particularly matters what you think," Quinn said, sweeping her hand toward the iron bars and locked door beyond. "Whether you believe me or not is pointless while I'm locked away. I have to decide if I want to risk my neck further by breaking out, or take a chance that Imogen is as smart as they claim."

Axe blinked. "You could get out?"

Quinn snorted, the corners of her lips turning up to smirk. "Do you really think I'd let them cage me and not have a way out?"

"Well, how am I to know you got other talents than what's between your le—"

"Finish that sentence and I'll remove your tongue," Quinn snapped. Axe's jaw snapped shut. She squinted at Quinn distrustfully.

"Fine," Axe wrinkled her nose and sniffed. "I guess you'd rather rot in here. But just so you know, *Madara* will be awake soon, and when she does . . ." Axe dragged a dirty finger across her neck, and Quinn rolled her eyes. "Unless you help me find proof against the person who did it."

"How do you know she'll wake so soon?" Quinn asked.

Axe pushed her lips together. "She will."

"She might listen to me," Quinn pointed out.

"Maybe," Axe shrugged. "Or maybe she'll have you and Lord Fierté hanged just to make a point."

Quinn grimaced, taking a casual glance over

the cell. Not that there was much of anything to look at, but she had to take a moment to let it sink in that she was going to align herself with a reckless pirate-child of all people. It was a dangerous move. A risky move. If the girl was right and her mother would indeed wake soon . . . Quinn needed to find Zorel fast. "If I help you, we do this my way."

Axe's brow furrowed. "Hold up now—"

"Uh uh." Quinn shook her head. "There's guards right outside of that door that I'll have to dispose of. Once the shift changes and they're unconscious with me gone, the bells are going to sound. If we're going to track down who poisoned the Queen, then you need to listen to me, otherwise one or both of us are going to get hurt—and even if I manage to clear my name, your mother won't look kindly on the person that got her kid hurt." Quinn pursed her lips, and the girl sighed.

"Fine, but when we find him, you don't get to kill him. Savvy?" Axe said. "He has to go before *Madara*, and her word is law."

"What makes you so sure she's going to live?"

"She has her ways," Axe answered cryptically. Her heartbeat picked up as Axe pushed off the wall and came to stand beside the bars. "Do we have a deal?" She extended a sweat-slicked palm smeared with dirt.

Quinn had to find and prove that the weasel had poisoned the Queen and then framed her . . . all while keeping him alive. While she didn't like it, she cared less for the consequences of killing him before he was brought before Imogen. Sacrifices had to be made, and there were other ways she could make him pay.

Ones that didn't involve death.

As she told Axe, there were worse things that could be done to a person.

Things that would make him wish she'd just killed him.

Quinn grasped Axe's hand, trying to ignore the sticky feel of her fingers. "Deal. Now about that door . . ."

The corner of Axe's red mouth curved up in a mischievous grin. She reached into her pocket and pulled out a set of keys bound by a silver ring. They jingled softly, and the sound trilled through the damp room. "I stole them off a guard on my way here," Axe said, unapologetically.

"Unbelievable," Quinn muttered, shaking her head. "But not necessary."

With a flick of her wrist, a wisp of fear took

form and shot toward the inner door of her cell. It slithered inside of the mechanism, and with a soft click, the bolt popped open.

The metal screeched as the iron door swung outward.

"What was that?" a voice said from the hallway. All laughing and joking stopped as Quinn strode forward. She reached for the latch, quietly undoing it. She couldn't hear them, but she could feel their fear as she opened the wooden door into the hall beyond.

Three guards stood there, white-faced and jaws hanging ajar.

"Hello, boys." Quinn grinned.

They didn't even have time to scream.

Questionable Actions

"The ends might justify the means, but that doesn't mean you have to like it."
— Quinn Darkova, vassal of House Fierté, fear twister, framed assassin

I n all of the possible scenarios Quinn envisioned for breaking out, hanging Axe from the third floor of the palace was not part of the plan.

With so many guards on patrol, they'd decided to avoid them and take another route to their destination. After knocking out the guards and scaling two walls, they climbed the steps to the third floor and made their way to the wing they needed.

Without an easier way down, Quinn was holding Axe out of a window in an empty bedroom, attempting to land her on the sill of the window below.

"Your hands are sweaty," the young girl griped. Quinn rolled her eyes to the skies, and for the tenth time in the last hour, she asked Lady Fortuna whether the girl's appearance in her cell was a blessing, or a curse, from the goddess of luck.

"Yes, well, running around a palace and scaling walls while trying to evade guards I'm not allowed to kill tends to do that," she replied impassively. Axe looked up, her tumble of red hair falling back as she glared at Quinn. The beads clinked in the blowing wind as she hung in the open air, swaying back and forth like a banner announcing their presence.

Quinn grimaced.

"I'm slippin', and this is a fifteen-foot fall. Do you want to tell *Madara* when she wakes up that you dropped her daughter out of a window?" Axe raised a brow.

"*Cunnus*," Quinn growled under her breath.

"What was that?" Axe stage-whispered loud enough to wake the courtyard.

"Nothing, *Your Highness*," Quinn replied, leaning

out further. Her abdomen curled around the sill, the hard wood biting into her stomach.

"Closer," Axe edged, swinging her feet to see if she could touch. "Almost there . . ." The movement made her wrists slip and one hand slid free. "Myori's wrath!" Axe yelled. Footsteps sounded down the hall as Ilvan guards said, "What was that? It sounded like the princess!"

"*Potes*," Quinn cursed. "Did you have to yell?" She leaned forward even further, nearly halfway out the window with a miniscule amount of space between holding onto the dangling girl and falling out herself.

"If your hands weren't so sweaty—"

"Gods be damned," Quinn snapped. She let go of Axe's other hand, and the girl let out a shriek as she dropped the last two feet. Her boots slammed onto the edge of the lower windowsill, and as she started to teeter back, Quinn was ready for her. With a sharp twist of her wrist, black tendrils slipped from beneath Axe's skin, pulled by Quinn's power, and they shot down to the girl's heels, solidifying beneath her.

Axe paused and looked down before looking back up at Quinn. Her hands gripped the wooden frame tightly as she narrowed her eyes.

"You could have told me you were goin' to do that," she hissed.

"Where would be the fun in that?" Quinn asked, leaning back to maneuver one leg out the window, straddling the frame. Footsteps came to a stop right outside the door behind her.

She was out of time.

Throwing caution to the wind, Quinn slipped her other leg over and let herself dangle off the edge. Wood banged against stone as the door was thrown open, and Quinn let go, falling and landing deftly at Axe's side.

"How'd you—"

"Shhh," Quinn whispered back, pressing a finger to the girl's lips. Axe eased to the side, giving her more room as the sounds of guards moving about in the abandoned bedroom drifted through the open window. Quinn leaned into Axe, pressing her lips to her ear as she said, "We need to get to the ground. I'm going to go first this time."

"But—" Axe started to cut in. Quinn shot her a glare, and she closed her mouth.

"I go first and then you follow. I'll catch you." The words had barely left her lips when Quinn turned and squatted. She let herself fall back on her butt, dangling her legs over the side as she did. Axe visibly quivered while watching her, but didn't protest again.

Quinn turned herself as she started to slide, maneuvering onto her stomach as she let herself hang and then fall, not able to waste precious time when the guards were already growing suspicious. Her boots hit the grass with a soft thump, and the rummaging two floors above her paused.

"Did you hear that?" one of them asked in Ilvan.

"Nothing's here," another said.

"Maybe, unless . . ."

Potes, Quinn cursed mentally. She was too loud. Someone noticed.

The floorboards creaked as someone started toward the window. Panic crossed Axe's expression as she wavered on the edge of the sill. Quinn motioned with her hands for her to jump. The small girl pushed her lips together, as if trying to stop herself from screaming as she stepped over the edge.

Her moment's hesitation was a moment too long.

A brown head peeked over the edge right as Quinn's arms came up to catch Axe. The awkward angle sent Quinn falling to the ground, still clutching the girl tightly. Her features were pinched together as they both waited for the inevitable yell.

But it never came.

The man squinted into the darkness, and Quinn stared down at herself.

Shadows wrapped around them, darker than the night itself. It seemed that even when her attention was split, her magic knew how to react the way they needed it to. Axe looked up, her brow furrowing once more as she peered into the murky darkness that surrounded them.

The guard shook his head once and turned away. "There's nothing down there."

"It must have been the wind," came a reply. Several of them chuckled.

"Send someone to check on the prisoner," said another voice. "Just to make sure."

Footsteps moved away from them, the sounds carrying out the open window to the ground below. Quinn exhaled heavily just as Axe said, "That was close."

"Yeah," she answered, pushing the girl off her. "No thanks to you."

"Hey!" Axe piped up as Quinn rocked forward onto her feet. She pressed her index finger to her lips, and the young woman pursed her lips, lowering her tone. "If you hadn't dropped me, I wouldn't have screamed."

"Oh really?" Quinn asked. "And what was the excuse for just now?"

She tapped her foot, tilting her head to the side while Axe spluttered for a moment. The girl shook her head before replying, "I don't have to answer to you."

Quinn snorted. "Right," she drawled, brushing past her and peaking around the side of the building. "How close did you say we were to Lorraine's room?"

"It should be just across from here," Axe responded, moving alongside her and poking her head out as well. Several feet away, a pair of guards strode past them, moving into the building through a side entrance. "Go," Axe hissed as soon as they were out of sight.

Quinn didn't hesitate. She sprinted across the opening of the courtyard and ended up pressed against the stone wall of the adjoining wing. Going out the window had certainly been faster, and they had avoided most of the places Ilvan soldiers would be patrolling. Axe's hand appeared in front of her face, pointing.

"That one," she said, aiming a few paces down

toward a darkened window with tightly sealed shutters.

"Are you sure?" Quinn asked. It would not be prudent to fall into someone else's room while they were searching for Lorraine, and though Axe had lived in this palace her entire life, Quinn still had to ask.

Axe nodded and slapped her chest. "I know this palace like a turtle knows the ocean," she replied.

Quinn took a breath and moved toward the window. She extended a hand forward. Black wisps drifted off her skin. They swirled in the air, forming obsidian threads that drifted down toward the seam of the shutters. Quinn wedged her fingers into the crack and helped hasten their entrance by pulling them apart, leaving the wisps to go to the inside edge of the glass pane.

"What are you doin'?" Axe asked at her side, eyes on the black magic at work.

"Opening the window," Quinn answered without breaking concentration. Right as the lock clicked and the window slid open, the blade of a sword appeared. The metal gleamed in the moonlight as it pointed directly at her chest. Quinn followed the length of it back to the man in the shadows.

A voice she recognized cursed in Norcastan.

"Dominicus?" Quinn stepped back as the weapons master stepped forward. Cutting blue eyes stared at her with disbelief.

"Lazarus sent me a message telling me that you'd been arrested for poisoning the Queen," he said, sheathing his sword. "What are you doing here?" His eyes cut to her side, and the scowl deepened. "And what are you doing with *her*?"

Quinn sighed. "I didn't poison the Queen. I was framed, but the only one who knows enough to clear my name is the person who actually did it. I came here because I need Lorraine's help."

He watched her for a moment, weighing her words and her worth.

"What information could Lorraine have that you would break out of prison for?" he asked, distrust plain on his expression and in his tone.

"I was the last person the Queen saw before she lost consciousness, and her symptoms looked awfully close to that day in the garden," Quinn said. The angles of his face were sharper beneath Leviathan's eye, revealing the lethal killer within.

"You think Lorraine was poisoned?" he asked.

Quinn nodded. "I do, and I think she might know what poisoned her."

Dominicus stepped back, leaving a gap big enough for them to climb through the window. Quinn nudged Axe, and the girl clambered over, stumbling forward into the dark room. Quinn followed, and the window clicked shut behind them.

"Lorraine still hasn't woken up," Dominicus started, moving through the dark room silently. "The healer assured me that she would, but then again, the healer also assured us that it was her wound opening back up. Not poison." A match struck, illuminating Dominicus' face. He lowered it to the oil lamp in hand, and a dim light spread enough for most of the small room to be visible.

In the corner of the room, tied to a wooden chair, gag in mouth, was none other than the healer.

Desperate Measures

"If you dance with Ramiel's patience, beware. Mazzulah's grace will also be preoccupied."
— *Quinn Darkova, vassal of House Fierté, fear twister, reluctant babysitter*

The fear permeating from her skin was enough to make Quinn's mouth water as Axe said, "Tell me you didn't kill my favorite guard."

Quinn paused in her assessment of the woman sitting before her and glanced back. Two Ilvan soldiers lay collapsed on the floor, no blood in sight. "They're unconscious," Dominicus answered stiffly as Axe knelt down and turned the prettier one's face.

"Well, as long as you didn't ruin the goods." She patted his cheek and then stood back up.

Both Dominicus and Quinn stared at her, perplexed at how to respond.

Strange girl . . .

"How's Lorraine doing?" Quinn asked, turning toward the bed. All she could see in this light was a pile of blankets.

"I'm not entirely sure," Dominicus answered. His fists clenched, and he shot a murderous look toward the healer. "I haven't been here long, but this one wouldn't stop screaming after I knocked the guards out. I had to tie her up and gag her just to get her quiet."

"But you didn't knock her unconscious either?" Quinn asked.

"Didn't want to," he muttered. "Not with Raine still asleep, but I also hadn't realized she lied to us either." The healer swallowed hard enough for all three of them to hear.

"Aw man, Harrietta," Axe said with a shake of her head as she switched to Ilvan. "I really hope you didn't do somethin' bad." The healer's eyes widened as she started to struggle, trying to say something to Axe. The young woman frowned and shook her head. "*Madara* was poisoned, and right now, the only person I believe didn't actually do it is her." She hooked her thumb toward Quinn. "I'm sorry, but if there's any chance you lied about their friend being poisoned, we don't know what else you lied about." Axe's expression hardened, and she looked at Quinn. Transitioning back to Norcastan, she said, "Do your black magic thing."

Dominicus quirked an eyebrow. "Her black magic thing?"

"Yeah, you know, the wispy shit that comes out and—"

"Not important." Dominicus shook his head, and Axe frowned. "Quinn," he motioned toward the woman.

She didn't need to be told twice. Quinn strode forward and came to kneel beside the woman, gently running the back of her hand over the stout healer's clammy cheek.

"I can make your deepest fears come to life," Quinn whispered softly in Ilvan. The scent of damp petals and fresh snow stirred in the air, though they were far from the cold. "I can show you things that will haunt you until you claw your own eyes out and still, you'll never be able to unsee them." The woman's eyes went wide as shadowy wisps of darkness rose from Quinn's skin and reached out. She flashed a vicious smile, and Harrietta shuddered. "Do you understand what I am and what I'll do to you if you lie to me?"

A brief pause. Harrietta nodded in jerky movements.

"Good. Now, I'm going to untie you, and if you scream, I don't need to tell you how much you'll regret it, do I?" The words fell from her lips just loud enough for the others to know she was no longer speaking Norcastan.

Axe gasped. "You speak Ilvan?"

"I speak many languages, but because of my skin, most people make assumptions about who I am and what I can do," Quinn replied without turning around. She could sense Dominicus' tension in the background, but at least in this she was the closest ally he had, and they both knew it.

Quinn reached up to yank the rag down under Harrietta's chin. The woman took two heaving breaths before pausing to glare up at Quinn.

"You're a black Maji," she spat in Ilvan. Quinn's smile widened.

"I'm a fear twister, yes, and if you don't cooperate, I have no problem using my magic to make you." Quinn quirked an eyebrow. "So, what's it going to be, Harrietta? You want to tell me why you lied to us, or do I need to take a walk through that mind of yours?" Harrietta pressed her lips together, and her already pink-tinged cheeks turned a shade darker in the dimly lit room as she inhaled deeply.

"I'll talk if the princess will grant me amnesty." Harrietta leaned as far as the rope would let her, attempting to look around Quinn to the child she clearly hoped would save her. Quinn glanced back at a scowling Axe.

"I don't have the power to grant amnesty, Harrietta. If you did somethin' bad enough you think you'll need it, you best start talkin', and I might ask *Madara* not to tie a stone to your neck and toss you in the bay. Savvy?"

Quinn swung her head back around, her lips lifting in approval as she eyed the heir to Ilvas. While strange she might be, Axe handled herself well for a child, and didn't buckle under pressure like most princesses her age might. Then again, she hailed from pirates. There's not a lot that tended to phase the bloodthirsty marauders who rode the waves of the sea.

Harrietta trembled, but there was a defiance in the stiffness of her shoulders. Her fear told Quinn that she knew what she was facing, and yet, the white Maji healer still tried to hold strong. It fascinated Quinn as much as it annoyed her.

"I was handed down orders that I thought were from the Queen herself," the woman said defensively. She licked her chapped bottom lip, wetting it. "I didn't know . . ." She trailed off, her gaze dropping as she shook her head.

"What didn't you know?" Quinn asked.

"I—" She hesitated. "I was told to treat your friend when she arrived. Two days later, I was approached by an advisor to the Queen and given"—Harrietta paused, as if she were trying to find the word—"different orders."

"Who was the advisor?" Quinn asked.

Harrietta only gave a brief hesitation before murmuring, "Lord Zorel."

Quinn cast a glance back over her shoulder at Axe, who was keenly listening.

"And those orders were?" she prompted as she turned back around, resting her elbow on the back of the chair.

"He gave me a vial and told me to sprinkle drops of it in with her tonic. That the Queen requested it." Something flashed through Harrietta's expression that Quinn expected, but she still didn't like it.

Guilt.

"What was in the vial?" she asked, her voice going hard as ice as she leaned into the healer's space.

Dominicus picked up on it and asked, "What did she say, Quinn?"

"The vial," Quinn repeated in Ilvan, ignoring him. "What was in it?"

Harrietta swallowed hard, her dry lips cracking. "I didn't know," she repeated. Quinn raised her hand, and the woman flinched. She stopped mid-air, her hand hovering as she curled her fingers inward. Black tendrils slithered up from her skin, sliding toward Harrietta.

"I will only ask once more," Quinn said coldly. The fear tendrils touched the sweat-slicked skin of her chin, and the woman contorted inward, squeezing her eyes shut.

"I didn't!" she exclaimed. "I swear I didn't know, not until—" She broke off, her eyes flying to Lorraine's bed.

"You told us she collapsed from her wound," Quinn said. The threads of fear danced over the tied-up woman's face, and she began to thrash.

"You told me to my face that she pushed herself too hard and she shouldn't have been out of bed, but that's not what happened, was it?"

"No, no!" Harrietta writhed, moaning in pain. Quinn pulled her hand back at the first signs of overload. The body could only take so much before it shut down, and the mind was no different. "I swear, I didn't know—"

"What was in the vial?" Quinn asked, her voice a deadly sort of calm. The kind of quiet that predators lurked in, and people were right to fear.

The healer sagged, and in a rasped whisper, she said, "Poison."

Quinn's eyes closed as she let out a harsh breath. She leaned away to give herself some space before she did something she'd regret.

"Why were you poisoning her?" Quinn asked, working her jaw to try to relieve the tension.

"I didn't know I was," the healer replied. "Not until she collapsed in the garden."

"You lied to me," Quinn growled. Dominicus was talking again. Asking her what the healer was saying, and everyone, even Axe, was ignoring him.

"I had just learned that I'd been giving her poison," the healer said in her own defense.

"And you didn't suspect anything was off when

you were given this vial?" Quinn asked in disbelief. "I don't buy it. Not even you, sheep that you are, could be so stupid."

The stubborn set of the woman's jaw made Quinn think there might be more to this little tale. She beckoned forth a single tendril to stir up her anxiety, and predictable as people always were, the healer talked.

"I had suspicions, but when you're a healer in this court approached by someone in direct contact with the Queen, you don't question it. Imogen's been known to behead people for less," Harrietta murmured, lowering her gaze as Axe started to move closer.

"*Madara* would never—"

"You're just a child. How would you know what your *madara* would or would not do to her subjects she thinks are disloyal?" Harrietta asked, raising her head once more. "Ask your Aunt Petra what happened to her previous first mate and then tell me that I should have questioned what was in that vial."

Axe's hand came flying through the air, and it was only Quinn's faster reflexes that stopped her. Quinn gripped the girl's wrist, suspending it mere inches from the healer's cheek. "One, if you're going to hit someone, make a fist. Only children and whores slap with their palms open," Quinn said. Axe clenched her fist, glaring at Quinn as she tugged her hand away. "Two, this is my interrogation. Take a seat, and you might learn something."

They stared at each other for several seconds before Axe broke eye contact and turned away, her arms falling to her side.

"Now," Quinn said, turning her attention back to Harrietta. "What was your next move after you knew it was poison?"

Shadows flickered over her salt-and-pepper hair as she leaned forward. "I went to Lord Zorel and asked him what was in it."

"And he said?"

She snorted once. "Holy water."

Quinn snorted too. It appeared he did have a sense of humor.

"When did you confront him about the poison?" she asked, crossing her arms over her chest. Dominicus had gone stone silent, likely because he'd realized he wasn't getting any answers until Quinn was ready to talk to him.

"This morning . . ." Harrietta answered, looking away again.

"What are you not telling me?" Quinn asked

softly. Her back ached, and her head was starting to buzz painfully from dehydration, but there wasn't much to be done about it just yet.

"I don't know for certain——"

"But you suspect . . ." Quinn urged.

"I *suspect* that I was not subtle enough in my inquiry," Harrietta stated, dancing around what she really meant.

"You think he realized you knew his orders hadn't come from the Queen," Quinn stated. Not a question, though Harrietta nodded as if it were.

"Y-yes."

"I see," Quinn murmured. If the healer was indeed telling the truth, then the Queen's poisoning might not have been some methodical attempt at murder, but instead a hasty attempt to cover his own tracks. "Do you realize that my friend showed the same signs as the Queen did when she collapsed, and given that you were in possession of the same poison that was likely used, this could end very badly for you?"

Harrietta spluttered for a minute. "I would never——"

"Poison the Queen?" Quinn inserted. "Perhaps not, but somehow the same poison given to you wound up in the Queen. I suspect if her alcohol were tested, any halfway decent apothecarian would be able to confirm with me."

The healer once again narrowed her eyes up at Quinn. "I didn't poison the Queen."

"I don't think you did," Quinn answered. "But the only way to clear my name is to find the person responsible. So, if you didn't do it, where is our assailant now?" Quinn lifted an eyebrow, and Harrietta blew out a harsh breath.

"I don't know where Lord Zorel's gone."

"And yet, no one else will be able to confirm your story, except you and him." Quinn shook her head and turned away from the woman tied to a chair. She looked at Axe and said, "We need to find him."

"I still don't understand why Zorel would poison her," Axe said, running a hand through her frazzled ends. "He wouldn't become king, and neither would any Norcastan Heir. *Madara* consumes poisons for this reason. She will have shaken it off in another few hours. He knows that."

"Which means his goal wasn't to kill her." Quinn ran her palm over her jaw, wiping away the sweat. "That only makes sense if . . . he wasn't after the throne at all."

"What do you mean?"

"I mean, all of this started with him poisoning Lorraine of all people." In the midst of a language he didn't understand, Dominicus' head looked up from Lorraine's prone form at the mention of her name. "Poisoning her makes no sense if what he wanted was the throne. If anything, all it would do is sow dissension between Lazarus and Imogen. If he found out that she were being poisoned at your Queen's command . . ." Quinn let that thought trail off, not even wanting to think about the chaos that would break loose if Lazarus had learned that. Then again, that may very well have been the purpose.

"Zorel was tryin' to pit *Madara* and Lord Fierté against each other."

"To prevent their alliance," Quinn said. "Except Harrietta was suspicious, so he poisoned Imogen to speed up the process and cover his tracks." She paused. "Myori's wrath," Quinn snapped, squeezing her eyes shut and letting her head fall back. "He's not here."

"What?" Axe jerked her head back, blinking twice. "Why do you say that?"

"You don't make an attempt on the Queen's life, knowing she's going to wake back up, and then stay in the same city." Quinn shook her head. "He's going to need a way out of here."

"The gates are closed. Nothin' in, nothin' out. We could wait him out—"

"What about the port?" Quinn asked. Axe froze, then let out a stream of curses.

"Quinn, now would be a really good time to tell me—" Dominicus started.

"Shh." Quinn pressed a finger to her lips, listening. The night was quiet with the exception of the howling winds, and in those brief pauses before it started up again, there was a pounding. Feet hitting marble over and over as soldiers made their way down the hall. They were still in the distance, but those footsteps were only growing louder.

In the next instant, a masculine voice rang out in Ilvan. "The prisoner is missing!"

It echoed down the halls, and Dominicus' expression scrunched. "What was that? What are they saying?" he asked.

Axe sucked the air between her teeth and said, "I think they just realized she's no longer in the dungeon."

"You have got to be—" Quinn's vision faded, and with it, her hearing. Black spots appeared in her sight, growing until they consumed it all. She blinked twice, and a distorted black and white version of Lazarus appeared.

"Quinn?" he asked. "You need to stay put—"

"I don't have the time for this," she growled, pulling back. Silently, she told Neiss, "*Tell him to buy me time. I know who tried to kill Imogen.*"

"*As you wish,*" Neiss answered.

The vision faded, and with it, so had her time. Footsteps sounded not far from the door, and she turned to Dominicus. "Watch over Lorraine and don't let anything happen to that healer. She's our way out of here." She thrust her head toward the window and said, "Axe, come with me."

Not needing to be told twice, the girl started for the window and slid it open, silent as the night. "Where are you going?" Dominicus asked in a harsh whisper.

"To catch a weasel."

To Track a Traitor

"Actions have consequences. Beware of the day you must pay the piper."
— *Quinn Darkova, vassal of House Fierté, fear twister, hunter of fools*

Tritol had gone silent—as if death's door were upon all of them, and not just Imogen.

For the first time since Quinn had arrived, not a single person was in sight. News must have traveled. Every tavern was closed. Every house was shuttered. If she didn't know better, she'd think it was a ghost town. But beyond the creaking of hinges and the howling wind, whispers carried on the breath of hidden strangers. Those whispers followed her and Axe as they strolled down the streets, masked by night, as soldiers walked on by, none the wiser to the two women that hunted among them. They couldn't hear the hushed voices of the people in those homes, but Quinn could. She could sense where they were with her field of vision as she scanned the area, empowered by their fear.

It was a heady combination; one that she couldn't allow to get the better of her when they did find Zorel. Much as she might want it to.

"So," Axe drawled. Her voice carried, too loud for the silence surrounding them. "How do you do it?"

Quinn glanced sideways, narrowing her eyes. "Do what?"

Axe motioned down the street to the group of guards that hustled on by. They looked directly at them, but saw nothing. Only darkness. It made getting around far easier when they didn't need to scale walls or jump from buildings. "That," she clarified, waving at the darkness.

"Illusions," Quinn answered, peeking her head around another corner before continuing on. "I mask us in shadows."

"But they're not real?" Axe asked, poking at the

murky black magic surrounding her. Her hand went harmlessly through it as the magic didn't respond.

"No." Quinn sighed, turning to look behind her and then back ahead. "Are you sure we're going the right way?"

Axe jutted her chin forward, pointing at the narrow alley. "Yeah, right ahead. We'll run straight into the shipyards." Quinn continued on, another minute passing before Axe started again. "Can you make illusions out of anythin'?"

"Define 'anything'," Quinn replied, only half paying attention as they approached the alley.

"Could you make them see a firedrake?" Axe asked, squinting her eyes with suspicion.

"Yes," she answered as the first sound of waves splashing the dock made its way to her ears. She took that as a sign to press forward and stepped in front of Axe, putting one hand to the cracked stone wall. The path was so narrow she doubted Lazarus could even fit between these two taverns.

"Really?" Axe asked, astonished. Quinn rolled her eyes, stepping around a leaking water pipe.

"Really," she answered, more tart this time.

"Can you show me? I've got to—"

"Shhh," Quinn whispered, turning to glare at her. "We're out here to find the person who's responsible for poisoning your mother, or have you forgotten?" Axe pulled her shoulders back and tied her bright red hair back with a leather cord. She gave Quinn a dirty look and pointed over her shoulder.

"You mean *him?*"

Quinn whipped her head around to see a dark figure scurrying across the docks. The humid air was thick with the coming storm, and the waves reflected the sky's melancholy, hammering into the rocks with enough force to send jets spraying the wooden planks. She saw him pull back his hood, muttering something under his breath Quinn couldn't quite hear as he took off his pack and tossed it up over the railing of the small ship he was clearly attempting to commandeer.

"Now listen," Quinn glanced back, opening her mouth to tell Axe how they were going to do this. There was just one problem.

Axe was gone.

Quinn turned, cursing under her breath. The alley was empty. Up ahead where the figure stood, trying to wrangle his way onto the boat while it rocked in the thrashing waves, there—to the side— was Axe. She moved lithely, making use of her small stature by staying close to the ground despite the torrent winds. Her cloak flapped around her as sea water sprayed, plastering the stray locks of her tangled hair to her face. She stalked Zorel as he reached for a rope, attempting to haul himself on board.

The advisor was about as strong as he was brave. Zorel cursed the sea as he shook, only two feet from the ground and still several more to climb before he would reach the deck. His arms trembled despite the minimal exertion, and Axe shook her head as she plucked a weapon from her belt.

Quinn saw her arm come up and began running.

The metal blade of an axe glinted under the hazy night sky.

Quinn put on a burst of speed, stopping just short of plowing into the girl's back, but she was too late. Axe's arm came down, and with it, the weapon flew. Sailing through the air, it spun in circles, picking up traction. Quinn tilted her head, watching as the hatchet careened forward, farther than a girl Axe's size should be able to throw. She'd expected it to strike him down as it closed on the distance in less than a second, but instead, it did the impossible.

The blade cut the rope as it swung in a wide arc.

Zorel fell at the same moment the weapon came sailing back through the air, into Axe's waiting hand.

She caught it with a diabolical grin painted on her lips. Zorel's decorative court sandals hit the docks and slid. He grasped the rope with a white-knuckled grip, but it did him little good when it was attached to nothing. His body pitched backwards, dropping to the wet planks like dead weight.

Quinn glanced between Axe and her prey with an approving nod.

"You can't kill him. We agreed," she said.

"I wasn't plannin' to," Axe replied without looking at her. "His punishment belongs to *Madara*." She raised her voice for those words to carry. Zorel trembled, struggling to stand up as one of his long sleeves got caught on a loose nail.

"Just making sure you remembered," Quinn murmured as the Queen's advisor looked up and squinted his eyes. "If I don't get to kill him, you certainly don't."

Axe sighed, giving Quinn a pointed look before starting toward him.

"Axelle?" he asked.

"Did you do it?" she called back, her voice lifting over the wind. He pulled frantically at his sleeve until it ripped. His gaze darted to the torn fabric and back to Axe, before looking onwards to Quinn.

He visibly paled.

Quinn smiled.

"What are you doing h-here?" he stuttered out, stumbling back. "Why are y-you together?" Axe continued walking, and Quinn followed, strolling leisurely behind her.

His fear was delectable.

It was taking all her self-control not to feast.

"Zorel," Axe said, her voice thick with emotion. "Did you do it? Did you try to poison *Madara?*"

"I—I—" He swallowed hard, his eyes flashing to Quinn as he attempted to get his visceral reaction under control.

Oh no, no. That won't do.

Quinn extended her hand, calling forth his anxiety. She could see it in his eyes, the way they glassed over as he started to spiral. Zorel was a weak one. She'd have to be careful not to break him before Imogen's questioning.

"I didn't do a-anything. I s-s-swear." His teeth chattered from a chill neither Quinn nor Axe appeared to feel. He rubbed his hands absentmind-edly, unaware or unable to fight the way his emotions reacted. "S-she did it." He pointed his finger at Quinn. It shook too much for his words to hold sway, and Quinn grinned to herself when Axe slapped his hand away.

"Then why did Harrietta tell us you poisoned their friend?" Axe asked him, looking into his sallow cheeks and beady eyes. He swallowed again, bumbling around his words.

"I—she—we—" Axe lost patience, and her fist went flying. She punched him in the mouth, and he blinked, shaking off his fear if only for a moment.

"You little bitch," he spat.

Zorel lunged forward with both hands, attempting to grab her, and Quinn tsked.

"That's enough of that," she said. With a wave of her hand, black tendrils wrapped around him, pulling his arms tightly to his body. He writhed under their confines, confused and terrified because he didn't understand.

Axe stared at him; her upper lip curled back in a feral snarl.

"You weak, lyin', skinny-legged, limp-walkin' bastard!"

Quinn's eyebrows inched up her forehead. "I've

never heard an insult quite like that one," she mused.

Axe kicked him in the stomach once for good measure, and he went falling again, banging his head on the dock. Quinn grabbed Axe's arm, hauling her back. "I can't believe I'm saying this," she said, looking to the cloudy sky. "But you can't beat him up. Not yet. Not until we bring him before your mother. All of my house are being held prisoners for attempted murder. Only he and Harrietta can prove we didn't do it."

Axe paused, glaring down at Zorel. His eyes were closed in pain. He moaned, but it wasn't earning him any sympathy.

"Fine." Axe shook her off.

"Now," Quinn started, "we need to find a way to get him back to the palace without making too much noise. Any suggestions?"

Axe shifted side to side before glancing down at the abandoned rope.

She bent at the waist and picked it up. Testing the thickness between two fingers, she pulled, and when it held, a dark glee entered her expression.

"I can think of a few."

Pressure's Peak

"Just as the Goddess Fortuna blessed some with luck, so too does Duessa give her favored duplicity."
— *Lazarus Fierté, soul eater, heir to Norcasta, impatient prince*

Lazarus clenched his fists, resisting the urge to reach forth and strangle the basilisk as he shook his slender head and dropped back to the floor. "*Quinn is busy*," the creature said. "*She asks that you buy her time.*"

Lazarus turned away, taking in Vaughn and Draeven. "What's that mean?" Draeven asked.

"She's obviously freed herself," Lazarus replied.

It was dangerous; but beyond that—it was reckless. A burning itch traced his spine, the souls beneath growing restless. The basilisk shrank away from him as if it worried that it would, once again, be pulled into him by his magic. Lazarus ignored the snake and strode across the room, turning sharply and retracing his path.

"Is she coming here?" Draeven asked.

Lazarus shook his head. "No, she's searching for the real assassin."

Draeven snorted. "She would." He leaned back in his seat and folded his hands behind his head.

"Dominicus should have my message by now," Lazarus said. "Perhaps if I sent another, he could—"

"Stop her?" Draeven interrupted, squinting his eyes. "You want to stop her? If she can find the real assassin, then that would be a good thing, wouldn't it?"

"It's reckless." Lazarus grit his teeth as a fresh wave of anger rolled through him.

Draeven stiffened as though he could feel the rage from his position across the room. "What else do you suggest, then?"

"You should do as she-wolf Quinn asks," Vaughn said.

Lazarus sent the man a scathing glance, but Vaughn did not heed the clear warning Lazarus intended.

"She will take care of this," he said with a nod. "We let her."

"I'm surprised you'd say that," Draeven commented. "Aren't your people more protective of their women?"

"She-wolf Quinn cannot be caged," Vaughn replied. "She is like animal. Wild. Untamed."

Lazarus paused in his pacing as Vaughn smiled fondly. As distasteful as the mountain man was, particularly his affection, he was right. Quinn was no innocent, ignorant to the darker facets of life. She *was* the darker facets of life.

Quinn could fight, arguably better than most. She could also track, but she knew when to disappear. In truth, this was what he'd trained her for. She was forged for this. If he put chains on her now, it would only set them back later. Instead, this would be a test; a show of her strength, and more importantly, her loyalty. He had no doubt that she could and *would* find the culprit behind the Pirate Queen's poisoning.

The real question was could she contain herself from killing?

Crossing his arms across his broad chest, Lazarus inhaled as he stopped at the window. He would exercise his patience, but should Quinn come to harm, should she somehow perish—whether by Imogen or her guards or even the assassin—Lazarus would unleash horrors upon Tritol unlike anyone on this continent had ever known.

But this was Quinn they were talking about. She had ascended.

The odds of her killing someone in a rage were far greater than her ever being killed.

All eyes shot to the door when the guards' voices just outside grew abruptly louder. A short pause of silence. They stiffened in anticipation as the door banged open and several men in blue and white uniforms filed in, only two with their swords drawn. A man stepped forward from the rest and gestured to the hallway behind him.

"You will follow," he commanded in Norcastan, his accent a thick-Ilvan drawl.

Draeven and Lazarus split a look between them, but neither attempted to speak as they nodded, and as a unit, filed out with the guards—Vaughn bringing up the rear and growling at any guard that dared venture too close. They were too busy watching him, squinting their eyes at Draeven, and trying to prod the mountain boy to bother noticing the shrinking serpent that had disappeared beneath a chaise. He had no doubts the creature would be returning to its master shortly now that its message had been received.

Paying no heed to the soldiers who kept their blades pointed at him, Lazarus followed behind the man who appeared to have some sort of authority over the others. He knew that should the guards attempt to harm him, they would be dead before their knees hit the marbled floors.

The same man who spoke stopped before the doors to the throne room and looked back with suspicious, untrusting eyes. "The Queen awaits."

The Queen?

Lazarus didn't show it, but he wasn't quite sure how Imogen managed to pull it off given what the basilisk had just relayed to him. She should be lying unconscious, somewhere near the brink of death. Yet, they were being brought before her.

The door opened and soldiers led them forward.

Imogen rested upon her throne; her skin bedewed with a light sheen of perspiration. She appeared shaken and pale, though her eyes were still sharp as cut obsidian as they watched him.

Lazarus noted the dampness of her gauzy white blouse and the slight tremor in her hands. While Imogen was out of the woods, she had indeed been poisoned and was unwell.

Lazarus walked forward, weighing his options. He would be a fool to think she would not notice Quinn's absence. That she would not know of Quinn's escape.

But to admit that he also knew, though he'd been under guard the whole time . . .

It would make her more suspicious than she already was.

"Lazarus Fierté of Norcasta," Imogen began. "It has come to my attention that a member of your house has attempted to take my life. How do you plead?"

Lazarus stiffened. It was then that he understood the basilisk's words.

Buy her time.

How much, he wasn't sure, but he would try. Lazarus feared nothing—least of all a death by the hands of the Pirate Queen—but he did not appreciate the way she curled her lip in distaste at the sight of him, nor did he like the clear disrespect her guards were showing his vassals as they jabbed at Vaughn and Draeven to drive them closer to him.

She wanted them together. Easier to slay, should the command be given.

Vaughn growled, ever the wild predator, and Draeven watched on, waiting for a signal of some kind. Lazarus would not be giving a signal, not yet. Instead, he tilted his head, looked away, and then back to the Queen, letting out a heavy breath. Imogen sat, her back straight and her legs spread to make room for the sheathed sword she held upright between her knees, its pointed end on the floor and the handle gripped in both of her fists.

Her intent was clear as she slid her hand along the long sheath. Her pointed nails tapped the fine leather, as if she were playing an instrument instead of impatiently awaiting his answer.

Lazarus dared not look away as he proclaimed, "Innocent." Imogen narrowed her eyes. "As my house is not responsible for your sudden illness."

Imogen lifted a brow in surprise. "Innocent?" she repeated. "You claim innocence in a time like this instead of admitting guilt and pleading for mercy? I'm not sure if I should be impressed by your gall or appalled by your lack of intelligence."

Lazarus nodded. "My house and I are innocent, Your Grace."

She shook her head. "You must be mistaken

about how this is going to go. I brought you here so that you may admit your folly before I strike you down." Her expression was hawkish, and her lips thinned as she stared down at him, already convinced of their guilt. "I will give you another chance to do so."

Lazarus remained quiet for a beat. With every second that passed by, his silence slowly crawled across her nerves and her ashen face grew pink with her anger.

Imogen stood, using her handle on the sword as grounds for her stability as she glared at Lazarus. "Admit your guilt, or I will have you burned alive and *her* skull placed upon a pike to be paraded through the country as a warning to those who lie in my court!" she shouted.

Lazarus lifted one elegant brow at her outburst. "I do not lie, Your Highness. My house is innocent of all accusations. If you look to your own house, you might find *more appropriate* suspects."

"My house?" She looked ready to unsheathe her sword and swing it at his head. Somehow, she managed to rein in the anger so plain upon her face. Imogen took a step back and retook her seat upon the chaise before casting a look out at those gathered before her. "My house knows that there is no way a poison could kill me. I've been ingesting different kinds from every land to dull my reaction to it for years. Only an outsider would attempt to kill me in such a cowardly manner."

"And you believe this outsider to be Quinn?" Lazarus asked.

"She was the one with me when I was poisoned," Imogen pointed out. The fingers that closed around her sword hilt whitened across the knuckles.

Lazarus shook his head, but as he opened his mouth to reply, Draeven spoke. "If you think Quinn is the type of woman to kill someone by poison, then you obviously don't understand her."

All eyes in the court shot to him—including the Queen's. "You are Lord Fierté's left-hand, are you not?" she inquired.

Draeven nodded. "I am, and Quinn is not your assassin."

The Queen sat back and eyed him before turning her gaze back to Lazarus. "You defend the N'skari with such passion," she said with a small smile upon her lips. "One might think there is more to the woman than meets the eye."

Lazarus' nostrils flared as a white-hot spike of rage sprung forth. It rattled the souls beneath his flesh, causing them to cry out and jerk in his skin—each one fighting to be released. After several moments of unanswered, tense silence, the Queen finally turned her cheek.

"It seems, however, that your N'skari is not the only one missing. My soldiers have informed me that Axe is also mysteriously gone. Care to explain that as well, Lazarus?"

The Queen knew very well Lazarus had nothing to do with her daughter's disappearance. Lazarus could see that very plainly without the help of his soul-stealing magic. Still, her eyes watched him with suspicion behind an inscrutable mask.

"I cannot speak for your daughter," Lazarus stated. "But I can assure you that no one in House Fierté had any hand in poisoning you. We have come here to strike an alliance. It seems counter-productive to attempt to kill the woman I would ask to align my country with, don't you think?"

Imogen's next words were a cold reminder. "You forget yourself, Lord Fierté. You are not a king yet." Lazarus gritted his teeth and remained silent. Provoking her would do nothing but raise his ire once more. Finally, she sighed and waved her hand. "If you have any proof, I would suggest you bring it forward now to present your case. I cannot promise mercy without evidence."

Lazarus and Draeven exchanged a look. "We —" Draeven began.

The loud scraping of the throne room doors being pushed in from the outside halted any further speech as Axe appeared, her shoulder-length hair haphazardly tied back. She shoved the doors open just enough for her and the person behind her to squeeze through before she started forward, striding across the stone flooring of the hall toward her mother, her head tilted back and an impish grin upon her face.

At her back, Quinn followed at a slightly slower pace, and when Lazarus saw the rope in her hands, he realized why. Struggling grunts emitted from the man—his wrists bound and attached behind him to his bound legs, another length of rope keeping them connected—as Quinn dragged him through the throne room.

Imogen's face was pure shock. Draeven stepped to the side as Quinn and Axe bypassed them. Quinn shoved her lavender hair back as she hefted the Queen's advisor onto the bottom most step of the throne and stood back with her hands on her hips. Axe beamed with pride.

KEL CARPENTER

"What's with the apple in his mouth?" Draeven finally asked.

Axe turned, and with her hands on her hips, answered, "He wouldn't stop talkin', so I thought we'd bring the pig in dressed up like one."

Quinn sighed and glanced over her shoulder. "She conned it off someone."

"Axelle," Imogen said. "What is the meaning of this?"

"This, *Madara*," Axe said, turning back to her mother, "is the *real* traitor."

Apple of Discord

"Neiss and Ramiel have always been friends; for where there is justice—there is also fear."
— Quinn Darkova, vassal of House Fierté, fear twister, assassin hunter

Imogen's shoulders straightened as she stared down at their evidence. Quinn and Axe stood with Zorel's body hog-tied between them. He struggled uselessly against his bindings, grunting as he tried to talk through the apple in his mouth. Finally, he managed to spit it out. Quinn looked down in distaste as it rolled to a stop in front of her feet.

"My Queen—" he began.

Axe bent down, snatched up the apple, and shoved it back in his mouth. "No talkin'," she snapped, clearly enjoying the feeling of power she had over the slimy weasel. He screamed in frustration and spit the apple back out. Axe bent down a bit slower this time, keeping her gaze locked on Zorel's as she picked it back up, but before she could shove it back in a third time, her mother interrupted.

"Axe," Imogen snapped. "Explain. Now."

Rolling back on the heels of her boots, Axe grinned. "We caught your poisoner, *Madara*," she said, gesturing to Zorel.

Quinn kept her mouth shut and took a subtle look around. More than two dozen Ilvan soldiers were gathered around the throne room, several of whom were surrounding the three men at her back. She felt Lazarus' fierce gaze on her, and for a moment, she turned, meeting his eyes. He wasn't happy. That was clear. Quinn turned back around and faced the Queen once more.

"Where is your proof?" Imogen demanded. "If you have brought my advisor before me with no evidence of his wrongdoing, then I'm afraid, *Tesora*, that you will be implicated in this mess as well."

Both Axe and Imogen looked to Quinn, and she

bit the inside of her cheek, looking around for her own proof. *Where in the dark realm is Dominicus with the healer?*

She knew she would have to make do until they arrived.

"We have a witness." Quinn cast a glance down, pressing her lips together to keep from grimacing at the man attempting to loosen the knots of his bindings with little success. "We also apprehended him attempting to *flee* your country."

Imogen's eyes turned down to Zorel, and without missing a beat, she switched to her native tongue of Ilvan. "Is that true?"

Zorel followed her example and spoke in slightly accented Ilvan as he responded. "My Lady—it's not what you think."

"Were you attempting to leave Tritol? To leave Ilvas while I was unwell?" she demanded. "It's a simple question, Zorel. Yes or no?"

"I-I was m-merely trying to . . ." He struggled and cut himself off as he yanked at his bonds. "For the love of Myori, will someone please release me from these blasted things!"

Quinn thought it interesting that he would plead for the love of Myori. The sea goddess held little love in her—much like the Queen herself.

Imogen nodded to Axe, and the girl huffed out a breath, pulling one of her axes from her belt. She bent down to saw at a few of the ropes until he could get himself free. Sliding the weapon back in place at her hip, Axe stepped back and pouted, crossing her arms.

Zorel cursed as he freed himself from the ropes and slowly stood, taking shaky steps toward the throne and away from both Quinn and Axe, but neither of them were having that. Together, they reached forward, each with a hand firmly grasped around one of his arms, and yanked him until he fell onto his knees on the bottom step of the Pirate Queen's throne. He took the hint and didn't move from his new position, but instead tried to beseech the Queen's forgiveness with his eyes. Quinn appreciated the flinty quality of Imogen's responding look.

"Your Highness, these two women are trying to frame me for your attempted assassination. I received an anonymous tip and—"

Heavy footfalls sounded behind the group. Imogen lifted her head, and Quinn followed her gaze as guards barked out commands. Dominicus strode forward, cold blue eyes homing in on Zorel. With one hand, he dragged the healer along beside him. Harrietta stared wide-eyed at the scene before her as soldiers halted their progression, waiting for an order.

With a wave of Imogen's hand, they backed away and allowed Dominicus to approach.

"Will there be more joining us?" she inquired tartly in Quinn's direction.

Dominicus was the one to respond. "No, Your Highness."

With a heavy sigh and a tightening grip on the sword between her legs, Imogen nodded for them to proceed. Quinn turned her attention downward at Zorel's panicked expression as he took in the appearance of Harrietta. His fear was palpable. *Delicious*. Quinn could smell it in her nostrils.

"I-I-I . . ." Zorel stuttered as everyone refocused on him. "Your Highness—this is highly inappropriate," he finally blurted. "To allow your suspected assassin so close to you and freed of her chains." He shot Quinn a glare filled with disgust and no small amount of anxiety. She returned the look with a lick of her lips, her pink tongue flicking out as though she could already taste his fear in her mouth. Zorel shuddered. Imogen watched him, waiting as he panted and heaved, overblown with fear and tight desperation. "She was found with your unconscious body in her hands, My Queen, surely that is—"

"Do you have more to present, Zorel?" she inquired.

He looked as though she'd backhanded him across the face. Quinn couldn't help but think she would like to see that happen. "Your Highness . . ." He blinked in shock. "I've been a loyal servant to your reign for *many* years. I would never . . ."

She lifted her hand, stilling his words as she nodded toward Quinn. "Now you."

Quinn gestured for Dominicus to bring the healer forward. He did so with a hard hand, releasing her arm and pushing against her back to urge her to stand next to the fallen Zorel.

"After you collapsed against me," Quinn began, her words flowing in perfect Ilvan. She could feel Lazarus' flash of surprise, followed by his seething fury through that strange quirk of magic she'd yet to understand, but she continued without turning, ignoring that his deep suction of darkness called to her as it touched her nerve endings and made her long for a little blood. "I was arrested. They sent me to the dungeons and while I was there, I got to thinking, Your Grace, about the uncanny timing of you being poisoned in the ten minutes I had been allowed alone with you." Quinn paused and extended her hand. A whisper of fear rose from her skin. "I wondered how it was that you came to be poisoned and who might benefit from it the most."

"If this is a means to distract me . . ." Imogen began.

Quinn allowed those tendrils to wind together and come to life, creating something that wasn't there. An illusion so grand, so real, so vivid, that the guards turned their weapons from Lazarus and his house to the great beast they believed to be in their walls. Guards gasped. Fear gripped all their hearts, men and women alike; all but two.

"My Queen—"

"Your Grace—"

The calls began at once, but it was Axe that spoke the loudest. "What's all this jabberin' about? Can't you lot see this is black magic?"

The room fell silent once more, taking in the firedrake that was not real, the girl that could see the truth, the hand at work, and the Queen who watched and weighed them all.

Quinn made the illusion throw back its head and roar once. The sound would have reverberated off the stone walls and through the ground itself, had it been real. As it was, the image disintegrated into black dust like ash, left to drift to the ground and disappear entirely.

"No," Quinn said, "they can't, but you can."

"What is the meaning of this?" Imogen asked. She didn't comment on Quinn's near-perfect speech in Ilvan.

"To show you that should I have wanted you dead—they would have never known. I could make them see and feel whatever I want. I could make myself invisible to all. I could kill you now, and not one of them could stop me," she said. Imogen's lips pinched together.

"Is that a threat?"

"No," Quinn answered. "It's simply the truth. If I, or Lord Fierté, wanted you dead, you would be. And they certainly would not have caught me." The court quieted for a moment, sensing that not all was as it seemed. Axe coughed, and the tension broke.

"Those are dangerous words to speak in my court," Imogen said, switching back to Norcastan. "You're either very brave or very stupid, and I can't quite decide which."

"Both," Draeven muttered lowly.

The Queen's lips quirked as she fought a grin.

"They are the truth," Quinn said, following her switch in tongue with ease. "Neither I nor my lord are so dumb as to be caught. We have the power to do as we wish, but we also have no reason to cause you harm. Lord Fierté came here to be granted an audience with you. He is seeking an alliance. To commit a shoddy attempt at murder would be stupid."

"Stupid?" the Queen repeated. Quinn nodded, the back of her neck damp with perspiration. "Very well. You've made your point, but you've yet to explain how my advisor is at fault."

"As I was saying, while I was locked away, I thought about who would have the most to gain by this play. Your advisor, Zorel, hails from Norcasta." She gave Zorel a pointed look, and the man gnashed his teeth, clearly wanting to speak the closer Quinn got to the truth. "Lazarus, as you already know, is fighting his own war with the noble heirs. It is not a stretch to think that the timing of you being poisoned was an act meant to drive a wedge between you and Lord Fierté—as it already has—and prevent any alliance from happening."

"You believe it to be the work of Claudius' blood heirs?" Imogen asked, her expression unreadable.

"I do."

It was a bold proclamation. Spoken to the

wrong monarch, it would be death. Quinn took a gamble that Imogen was a smarter woman than she was prideful.

Silence spanned the length of the marble throne room while they waited for her response.

"Lord Fierté," she said eventually.

"Yes, Your Grace?"

"Do you believe there to be any truth to this claim?" the Queen asked. Quinn didn't move an inch, nor did she allow her muscles to tense while she listened.

"I believe there"—she felt his eyes on her back, boring into her with that shadowy dark gaze—"to be a possibility, if you will. I cannot say for certain, but Quinn is not alone in her musings."

"That's what they want you to think, Your Highness," Zorel interrupted harshly. "These people are foreigners—outsiders—and they speak nothing but lies."

"You forget, Zorel," Imogen said, ice in her tone. "You too were once a foreigner, as the N'skari girl has so nicely pointed out." Zorel choked but didn't respond. Quinn let out a breath, her chest falling as her eyes rose. Imogen was staring at her. "Do you have more than musings to back up this claim?" the Queen asked. "Do you," she looked at her daughter, "do either of you have any proof?"

"Your Grace, Lorraine—my fellow vassal—was afflicted with a similar illness a few days ago," Quinn said. "She collapsed the same way you did. I told Axe as much when she broke into the dungeon I was being kept in, and when I broke free, we both set out to find my companion and see what she knew. Instead, I found your healer. I interrogated her and learned the truth." Quinn looked to healer Maji as she trembled before her audience.

"Is this true, *Tesora*?" the Queen asked her daughter in Ilvan.

"Yes, *Madara*." Axe nodded.

"Helping her escape was reckless. If she'd killed me for my throne, she might have killed you too . . ." Imogen's words trailed off, a painful expression briefly flitting across her features.

"But she didn't," Axe pointed out stubbornly.

"But she didn't." The Pirate Queen nodded, looking away for a moment before turning back to the healer before her and the matter at hand. "Harrietta," the Pirate Queen called. "What is the truth that she speaks of?"

"I-I didn't know, Your Highness," she stuttered in Ilvan. "I'm so sorry. I had no . . . the poison . . . it was . . ." The healer broke down, sobbing uncontrollably as she fell to the floor under the weighted stare of the members in the court.

"Lorraine didn't collapse because she reopened her wound," Quinn said with an irritated glare at the healer, speaking in Norcastan for her own house's benefit, namely Lazarus. "She was poisoned."

Imogen looked to the healer. "Is this true?"

Harrietta nodded, and through her sobs, answered, "I w-was given a vial, Your Highness. I was asked to add it to the t-tonic. After the woman's collapse, I approached—" She broke off, her weeping overpowering her for a moment. "I t-thought it was by your command, my Queen. I swear it." She lamented, bowing low over the stairs of the throne.

Quinn looked down at her scuffed boots and grit her teeth. She was beginning to grow tired of her wails.

"And who gave you this vial?" Imogen asked.

"Your a-advisor, my Queen," Harrietta cried.

The Pirate Queen stood, appearing stronger despite her pale face and shallow features. The dark circles beneath her eyes didn't pull so tightly at her skin as she descended the steps of her throne, using the sword in its sheath as a cane until she stood before the shaking Zorel.

"Do you have anything to say to this, Zorel?" the Queen inquired.

When the man stubbornly kept his mouth shut, Quinn stepped forward. "May I?" she asked. Tendrils of darkness slid from beneath her skin, racing down her arms and dropping from her fingertips before reaching for the advisor, but Quinn held them at bay, waiting for Imogen's response.

"What will you do to him?" the Queen asked curiously.

Quinn let a hint of the darkness creep into her voice as she said, "I'll make him tell you the truth."

"But you're not a truth spinner," Imogen replied. It wasn't a question, but a statement.

"No," Quinn said, "I'm much worse. I'll prey on his fears, and he'll spill his every thought just for me to stop."

"If I hadn't seen the illusion of the firedrake I might not believe you," Imogen said. "But I did. Show me, Quinn of N'skara, vassal of House Fierté. Show me what you can do."

"Gladly," Quinn whispered, knowing that she would finally be able to deliver his treatment of her in kind.

Zorel gasped as the tendrils touched him, and he jerked in their grip as his eyes grew large. Throwing his head back, he cried out. Veins began to pop at the top of his forehead as Quinn forced her power into his mind and cracked it open. She sought the truth, and he would tell them.

"Did you poison the Queen?" Quinn asked quietly. She whispered intimately, like she would to a lover.

"Yes," he choked. "Yes—I poisoned the bitch—Gods above—make them stop." He scratched at his arms, his chest, his face. Blood welled on his skin and crimson quickly soaked the beds of his finger-nails. Imogen watched Quinn with interest before flipping her scrutiny to the man writhing on the ground at her feet.

"Why?" Imogen asked. "Why did you poison me?"

"I was told—" He choked up, his hands wrapping around his own throat. "I was told . . ." he repeated, weaker than before. He was trying to get the words out, but something prevented him. Quinn set a flicker of fear free, and it broke apart, slithering across his skin like an inchworm. It encircled his wrists and pulled them down and behind him. The black tendrils locked together behind his back, and Zorel bent forward, sobbing into the marble steps.

"Why did you poison me?" Imogen repeated.

"B-because"—he paused, breathing heavily —"because I was told to."

Imogen's features revealed nothing. Her face was void of emotion, but her anger—Quinn didn't need eyes to see and feel that. She was made legendary for her wrath. Traitors were eviscerated in her court. Their corpses strung up in the streets for the crows to pick at and for all to see.

"Who told you to?" the Queen asked.

Zorel shook with fear. A wet spot appeared on his trousers and spread, dampening the floor. Quinn wrinkled her nose at the smell of piss, eyeing him like a bug beneath her boot.

"I can't say," he moaned. Imogen leaned forward, and though she hid the wince well, Quinn could tell she was in pain.

"Who told you to poison me?" she asked again. "Anyone in the closest circle of my court knows that poisons do not affect me as they do others," Imogen said, staring down at the top of Zorel's head as he bent at her bare feet. "It would not have killed me. You know that. Yet you did it anyways, and I can't help wonder who would dare infiltrate my court in such a bold and foolish manner." Her voice was little more than a hiss of air between her teeth by the end of it. Zorel would not answer, though. He would not say any names.

"I can't tell you," he moaned. "He forbade it."

"He?" Imogen asked, her flat gaze sweeping up to Quinn. "Who is he talking about?"

Quinn looked down at the advisor that dared frame her. Her fingers curled slowly, the joints tightening as her fingers contorted. She pulled on that power in her veins and looked deep into his mind.

"I see a man," Quinn started. "A man . . . with a cane." She frowned, because this wasn't the first time she'd seen his face. It had been well over a month, but on a dark road in the middle of the night, she saw a brief flash in another man's mind. A mind that had been consumed by fear as Lazarus killed him for attacking them in a carriage bound for Shallowyn.

"Can you get his name?" Imogen asked.

A phantom laugh rang in her ears—more viscous, more mad than anyone she had ever seen.

"No," Quinn said, trying and failing to search for more. "But I can tell you what he looks like."

"Do it," Imogen demanded.

The words spilled forth from Quinn's lips.

"His hair is silver, not like mine—but from age. One eye is brown and the other, clear. He has a scar running down the left side of his face that looks like —" Quinn broke off, pulling away from the vision in the man's mind.

"Looks like what?" Imogen asked.

Quinn turned and regarded Lazarus. His expression was closed off. His eyes burning with dark flame. She wondered what would happen to the world when he turned those eyes to it. Would it catch fire as her blood often did? Would it withstand? Or—would it all simply go up in smoke?

She shook her head and looked away.

"It looked like someone had cut him. I don't think he has use of his eye." On the floor between her and the Queen, Zorel descended into a blubbering mess of madness, causing Quinn to draw back her power before it completely broke his mind. He closed his arms around his shoulders, rocking back and forth as she wondered if she already had.

"I see," Imogen said, looking between Quinn and Lazarus. Axe stepped forward; her pointed chin turned upward.

"He's confessed, *Madara*," Axe said. "Surely, this is proof enough."

Imogen nodded quietly, contemplating her next

actions. "I never got a name out of him, but it doesn't matter, I suppose. We deal with all traitors the same." With one hand holding the sword by the scabbard and the other firmly around the hilt, she slid the blade from its resting place.

"Can we roast him?" Axe asked. It was enough to pull Imogen from whatever ghost Quinn had sworn was haunting the Queen's eyes.

Imogen shot her daughter an amused but reproachful glance. "We're pirates, *Tesora*, not cannibals."

Quinn frowned as Axe crossed her arms, turning to face Zorel alongside her mother. She pouted even now, sullen at the idea of not getting to eat him. *What a strange child . . .*

Imogen stuck the very tip of the blade under his chin. Zorel blanched, his face leached of all color as he tilted his chin back further to avoid the dangerous edge.

"Zorel of Ilvas, you have confessed and been found guilty of treason against your queen," she announced. "Do you have any last words?"

He opened his mouth—as if ready to give one last pitiful attempt at defending himself—but she didn't wait for him to speak. Imogen thrust the blade through the skin of his throat. Zorel's eyes bulged, and his arms dropped limp to his sides as the sword cut straight through cartilage and bone, the metal tip pointing out the back of his neck. Scarlet dripped from the end of the blade and dribbled down his body, seeping into his tunic. His mouth gaped as he gurgled, clinging to life like a fish struggling to breathe.

Imogen pursed her lips. "Traitors don't get any last words. You should know that," she said, placing her foot on his chest and pushing him back. The movement seemed to take all of her strength and as she stepped back, struggling to keep her balance. Axe moved forward, tucking an arm around her mother's waist to support her weight as the slight tremors of the poison persisted. Zorel fell onto the ground and into the steadily growing pool of liquid surrounding him.

Piss and the tang of copper filled her nostrils as she and House Fierté and all of the Pirate Queen's court watched Zorel die a traitor's death.

Sticky streams of blood ran free, staining the marbled floors. Quinn followed those lines to the toe of a black boot. Lifting her head, Quinn met Lazarus' eyes. His gaze let her know they were not finished here. That no matter what Imogen might declare, she'd seen and done things that day that he wouldn't forget. For good or bad . . .

"Quinn of N'skara, vassal of House Fierté," Imogen announced, drawing their attention back. "You are hereby cleared of all accusations."

She nodded and stepped back as Axe led her mother away from the body. When the Queen passed Lazarus, she paused, and they spoke quietly. Quinn frowned, trying to make out their words. Axe smiled over her mother's shoulder at Quinn and winked.

In a louder voice, Imogen turned and spoke again to the soldiers gathered. "House Fierté is released from arrest. They are welcome in my palace, to come and go as they please as friends of the crown." Several of the guards glanced at one another, but then relaxed, sheathing their swords. "We will speak at another time, Lord Fierté." He nodded and bowed his head respectfully, as did the rest of the room while Axe and the Queen left them.

Something moved in the periphery of her vision. The apple. From the bottom step, it tumbled, rolling through the blood all the way to the edge of Quinn's boot. Crimson coated its dark red outside, but the bite mark showed the white flesh of the fruit, slowly soaking up the droplets that slipped from the skin downward. Zorel had been an advisor to a Queen and a pawn to another man somewhere on this continent.

In the end, though, the only mark he left in the world was the bite in an apple that would wither and die in the juices of a man that had learned just what it meant to oppose a force of nature.

Something Wicked Comes This Way

"Cautious men are living men. It is the heroes that don't survive war."
— *Draeven Adelmar, vassal of House Fierté, rage thief*

S weat beaded on the back of Draeven's neck as he passed through the corridor. A battalion of palace guards strode by in pairs, many of them straightening at the appearance of the foreigner. Draeven sighed, his steps slowing as he reached back and scrubbed the palm of his hand over the damp nape beneath his hairline. It was unfortunate that the people of Ilvas now feared most of Lazarus' house, but it was also not surprising. After

Quinn's performance in the throne room, he doubted if there was a soul in the Pirate Queen's palace that had not heard of House Fierté and the dark Maji that they possessed.

Stopping before Lazarus' door, Draeven glanced down at his hands and took a breath, unclenching his fists. It would not do to let the stress of circumstance affect him so heavily. He needed to keep a logical head, because sometimes he was the only one trying to do so—ever since Quinn showed up.

Lifting his hand, Draeven knocked three times before he stood back and waited. Within moments, Lazarus' voice filtered out, strong but emotionless.

"Come in."

Draeven grimaced at the hard tone that suggested a sour mood, but nonetheless, he twisted the handle and entered. Lazarus sat by the fireplace in one of the twin wing-backed chairs positioned there. Closing the door at his back, Draeven walked farther into the room until he was standing before his master—the man he had chosen to follow and obey, though in the deepest recesses of his heart and soul, he knew it would mean an eternity in the dark realm come his demise. Lazarus was not a man built for good. He was built for power.

Draeven realized that fact; acknowledged that following this man was necessary if the ways of the world were going to change. Sacrifices had to be made, and if one of those sacrifices had to be his soul . . .

Then so be it.

"What news do you bring me?" Lazarus inquired.

"Quinn has returned to her room. Dominicus is back with Lorraine. She is recovering well and should be ready for light travel within the next few days," Draeven said.

Lazarus sat back, an empty crystal decanter dangling loosely from his right hand. In the fire-light, the thin white scar on the side of his face was enhanced, setting the rest of his features in shadow and not giving Draeven any hint to his master's current mood. "The journey to N'skara will be at least a week," Lazarus finally said. "By ship, hope-fully, but I would not consider that light travel. It is no leisurely ride by coach in the country."

"I understand," Draeven replied. "I said as much to the healer, and she suggested that we travel by ship and keep Lorraine confined to a bed for the journey. She shouldn't be moving about for another three days minimum. This is all just precautionary measures to ensure that her wound doesn't reopen again."

Lazarus' jaw clenched in displeasure, but there was nothing more either of them could do. Lorraine had already made considerable improvement, and now, it was up to time to heal her wounds. Time was not something they had in spades.

"What else?" Lazarus asked. "You would not come to me this late at night for a mere update on the others. What do you wish to get off your chest?" He gestured with his glass. "Say what you will."

A grimace graced Draeven's lips. Lazarus was right. "Sir, with all due respect—"

"Save the formalities for the court, Draeven," Lazarus interrupted, shooting him a reproachful glance.

Draeven bowed his head slightly before nodding and straightening once more. His violet eyes hardened as he stared down at the man who had given him power and purpose, who had taught him the strength in loyalty. He had never questioned Lazarus . . . before now.

"Quinn's vision," he started. "The man she described is familiar." The edges of Lazarus' lips tightened as a scowl threatened to overrule his stoic expression. Draeven continued. "You know that he's not one of the blood heirs. We both assumed—"

"I'm well aware of the situation," Lazarus interrupted once again. "And I'll warn you not to assume a thing until we have further information."

"Lazarus," Draeven spoke his name as he dropped his arms from behind his back. "There's no possible way she could know who she was describing."

"No," he agreed. "She likely doesn't."

"If *he's* involved with the blood heirs, then something has to be done. And sooner rather than later," Draeven said. "To put this off might mean the demise of your reign before you even claim the crown."

Lazarus was already shaking his head before the man was finished. "I will claim the crown regardless of any involvement he may have. Worry not over that."

"I think we should return to Norcasta . . ." Draeven argued.

"No, we will continue to N'skara. We cannot go back until we have everything we've come for." Lazarus stood and circled the chairs, heading across the room toward the glass bar where a container of amber liquid rested. Draeven tracked him with his gaze.

"The risk is too great," he warned.

Lazarus chuckled, the sound a cold and sinister thing. "Risks abound, Draeven. So long as the blood pumps through my veins, there will never be a moment of peace. Risk is what the world runs on; it is what people like me thrive on. If there is a risk too great for me—in N'skara of all places—then perhaps I don't deserve to be crowned king." He turned abruptly and fixed Draeven with a stare. "But there isn't, there won't be, and I *will* be King. Through blood and fire, I will remake this world, Draeven. Make no mistake. There is no man nor creature that can do what I will."

His words were powerful. They were the very words that had first convinced him to lay his sword and his life down at Lazarus' feet. Even now, it was hard not to yield entirely to his master's conviction and let the subject drop.

"I follow you, Lazarus, and I will continue to do so until the day my soul meets Mazzulah's realm," Draeven whispered the words as Lazarus raised his fist and gulped down a healthy portion of his drink. "By the gods, if *he* is involved"—Draeven broke off and let his gaze meet Lazarus'—"then make your plans now. I rather like living."

Lazarus' face remained aloof. "They are made," he finally said. "I will meet with Imogen and work out an alliance with Ilvas. We will travel to N'skara, obtain our objective, and then we will return to Norcasta to await Claudius' passing."

Draeven sucked in a breath and gave a weary nod. There was still a heavy bit of concern weighing his mind, but with Lazarus' decision made, he had no more to offer. Whatever happened, he would be prepared. He had to be.

Just as he turned to leave, Lazarus spoke again. "There is a reason N'skara is so important, Draeven," he said, causing Draeven to turn back to him. His lips parted as he regarded the way Lazarus lifted his half-empty decanter and raised it up, letting the light from the dancing flames in the hearth flicker over the pretty clear surface. "There is something there for her. Something she has not revealed. I find myself curious . . . if not suspicious as well. Whatever happens beyond this—in N'skara —I believe will be a turning point. I will have her loyalty, and with it, I will cement my reign."

Draeven considered this. A part of him should have known that there was more to Lazarus' insistence of traveling to N'skara, and it did not surprise him that part of that reason was because of Quinn.

He knew why Lazarus believed the N'skari woman was so special; why his master craved dominion over her. With Quinn, he would be capable of a great many things. With her, he would become what he was meant to be.

The dark heir meant to change the world for the better.

Or for the worse.

Either way, the change was coming, and not a soul could stop it.

Not even him.

Glass Palaces

"Those in glass palaces should take care."
— *Lazarus Fierté, soul eater, heir to Norcasta, unbending prince*

Lazarus stalked the corridor, following behind the guard that had called for him. The soldier seemed nervous. He walked too fast, and he kept turning his head just slightly, as if making sure that Lazarus were still there. Perhaps it was Lazarus' dark mood; perhaps it was something else. It could not be denied, however, that when the guard showed him to the Queen's private chambers, he was relieved to be finished with his duty.

"Come in," Imogen's voice called from beyond the doors.

Lazarus reached forward and turned the handle, stepping inside the hazy interior. The Queen reclined back on one of her infamous lounges with a pipe held out. Lazarus didn't blink as the plumes of gray poured from between her lips, nor did he wave away the smoke wafting toward his face—though part of him desired to. While he drank like the pirates, he didn't care for the mind-numbing herbs they turned to in pain or sadness. Imogen knew that, and still, she grinned up at him.

"You called for me."

"Yes, I did." Imogen gestured with her free hand. "Have a seat, Lazarus. I've decided to grant you your audience." Lazarus sat across from her as a side door to the chamber opened and a servant, as equally nervous as the guard had been, entered. Imogen signaled for the girl to move closer. "Do you want anything to drink?" Imogen asked.

"Spirits," he replied, his answer short and succinct. It would make the games he had to play with her easier. Less strained.

The Queen nodded and flicked her hand, sending the servant scurrying across the room and back out the door. Moments later, she returned with a crystal glass and a decanter of amber liquid that she set down on the intricate table between them.

"Thank you, Pilar," Imogen said. "You may go."

The servant bowed low and scrambled to get out of the room without dallying.

"Your servants seem a bit uncomfortable around me now," he commented lightly, reaching for the decanter and pouring himself a hefty amount. "Is there a reason for that?"

Imogen laughed. In the day or so since Zorel's death, she'd recovered from her poisoning with a constitution that befit a Pirate Queen. Still, she must have been feeling some of the residual side effects if she was openly using the herbs imported from the Crystal Continent. He sniffed the air. He had heard tales that the stuff could reduce any pain —mental or physical.

"My people have always been nervous around you," she said, drawing his attention back. "They simply hid it better before. Now, they recognize just what kind of power you wield."

Lazarus' hand stilled with the glass halfway to his lips. "And just how would they be able to ascertain that?" he inquired, his grip tightening. There was no possible way that they could know the truth.

Imogen inhaled deeply, her chest expanding before lowering as she exhaled more smoke. "Your girl put on quite a show in the throne room," she stated, "and people talk. They're calling her the white raksasa and you, her dark master." She chuckled at that, and Lazarus felt his tension ease.

"I can assure you, though she's a dark Maji, Quinn is entirely human." Lazarus sipped his drink and held the burning liquid on his tongue for a brief moment before swallowing, savoring the richness of it.

"Oh, I believe you speak the truth, but their whispers have merit. Quinn is a special one. I wish I had her for myself." The scent of the Queen's drug seemed to thicken in the room as she exhaled and blew out a stream of smoke. "If I thought it were possible to pull her away from you, I would have already done so."

Lazarus muscles tightened once more. He did not like the thought of Quinn under anyone else's control. "Did you call me for an audience to talk about my vassal or was there more?" he asked, deflecting her interest.

Imogen eyed him as she set her pipe down and crossed one thigh over the other, her dress splitting open to near-indecent levels. Lazarus kept his gaze upon her face as her chin tilted to the side, and she stretched her long neck. "Yes, your request," she said and then quieted as she sighed. "You wish to make an alliance with my country."

Lazarus nodded. "I do," he said. "An alliance between the strongest rulers is imperative to my plan. It will be the largest coalition the continent has seen since ancient times."

"What's in it for me?" she asked, and she laughed at his raised brow. "Come now, Lazarus, you didn't think you could enter the glass palace for nothing?"

"That's a rather old saying," Lazarus replied.

She continued to chuckle. "Yes, from an old story." When she didn't go on and Lazarus waited expressionless—hiding his emotions—she folded her hands over her lap. "Do you recall it?" she asked.

"I've never heard it in its entirety," Lazarus admitted with cool detachment. "But I don't understand what it could possibly have to do with our audience."

Imogen's lips parted, her teeth gleaming in the soft candlelight as she found his words amusing. "As you know, the glass palace is the tale of the greatest treasure gifted by the gods. Demoor—the creator of land—constructed it himself. Only those with honorable intentions could enter, and they were gifted with the power of magic by Vissilez. Everyone else was cast out as unworthy. Surely you know this is how Maji were created?"

Lazarus sipped from his glass, keeping sharp eyes on the dangerous woman across from him as he slowly nodded to her question. "I'm aware that many believe that."

"It's an old tale, passed down through the generations, but never written." She smirked as she eyed him. "You'd be surprised the stories you hear aboard a pirate ship, Dark Prince."

He returned her grin, though it didn't meet his eyes, and he lowered his glass. "I doubt there is anything you could say that would truly shock me."

She shook her head, smiling to herself. Lazarus narrowed his eyes, and Imogen spoke again. "There are many things I know, and some would probably do more than shock you. I've lived a long life for a pirate, even longer for a Queen. But that is not why I called you here today." She took another puff of smoke and coughed twice before the haze took her. Her eyes glazed over with a dazedness that indicated the strength of whatever she was smoking. "The point is that glass palaces represent transparency and honesty"—she paused for a moment —"truth." Lazarus lifted his glass to his lips once more. "And those things are rewarded. If you want alliance with me, you'll have to first prove yourself worthy."

"No amount of money could prove my worthiness," Lazarus said.

She nodded almost absentmindedly, slowly blinking and then turning her bloodshot gaze toward him once more. "Only the truth can do that. So, be honest with me, Lazarus. What do you seek?"

"You must understand that an alliance benefits all parties involved. I've brought the Ciseans into my fold. Now, you. Then, N'skara."

Imogen chuckled. "If you think N'skara will be as easy as declaring them your allies, then you're sorely mistaken. Those prigs are nothing if not tight-fisted in their ways. They like outsiders even less than the Ciseans." Lazarus could not deny that, but with Quinn . . . his carefully laid plans were bound to turn up results. He would accept nothing less. "Why do you want an alliance, Lazarus?" she asked. "Truly. What is it that you fear? Do you worry that Claudius' blood heirs will try to take the throne from you the moment their father perishes?" She let her gaze trail over his body; her eyes lighting as she took him in. "I'm sure you can find some way to pull them under your control. They are mere children, after all. Toss a few gold coins their way— a few women—and they will amuse themselves." Her eyes slid sideways as she let out another puff of smoke. "Or just kill them." She huffed as if that should've been obvious. "I'm sure a man such as yourself would have no problem accomplishing the task. For the love of Myori, send your white raksasa. I'm sure she'd enjoy the challenge—if she finds it challenging at all, that is."

Quinn would certainly enjoy that. She seemed to take great pleasure in holding power over those she crushed beneath her boots, and Claudius' children would likely be no different. Perhaps she'd enjoy taking their lives if she were informed about their particularly unique way of dealing with their slaves. But Lazarus couldn't yet allow her to have that kind of choice. He would not disrespect Claudius by killing his blood heirs until the old man had left this world and entered the void of the deceased. And even after his friend's death, Lazarus knew he would do what he could to keep the blood heirs alive. Their presence in court kept the common people docile, and more importantly, the lords. If a man such as himself with no birthright could become king, who else would get it in their mind to try such a thing before his crown was even secured? No. At present, despite their irritating antics, they were more valuable alive than dead. When that changed, he would reevaluate . . . but not until then.

"Every man wants power, Imogen," Lazarus said, finally allowing himself the use of her given name. "They will be no different, but they are not the sole reason for this alliance. With a bond between the primary powers of the continent, an era of prosperity is bound to happen, is it not?"

She waved her hand. "Ilvas is already prosperous," she pointed out.

"For now." The weight of those two words gave Imogen pause as she set aside her pipe.

She narrowed her eyes. "What do you know?" she asked, her tone sharpening.

Lazarus could feel an itch under his skin. Imogen's cheeks were pale, but the circles beneath her eyes had lessened. Despite the dulling drug, her disoriented gaze had an alertness to it. An intensity that told him despite its presence, despite her looks, she was very much paying attention to what he had to say. "The changing of sovereigns only happens so often," he said slowly. "As you well understand, there is a new era of rulers approaching. Both with you and with myself. You are royal in power and strength, but not in blood. The same is true for me. Surely, you must see the position we're all in."

"You're including the others in this? Jibreal? Bangratas? Even Triene?" Imogen looked startled and then thoughtful. "I have heard of the situation in the southern region. They are rumored to be changing rulers. You're right; the power of the world is shifting hands."

"Regardless of the southern region," Lazarus began, "and all propriety and nonsense aside, you owe me this alliance, Imogen."

She blinked once; any disorientation disappeared instantly as her sharp, keen eyes stared him down. "I owe you *nothing*, Dark Prince," she replied, her voice dry and brittle like the leaves she smoked. "You were paid handsomely for your services."

"And you know very well you wouldn't have this throne without me or those *services*." He took one sweeping glance around the room, taking in the lush opulence. "How much was it that you stole from the emperor's coffers? Surely enough to build your own dynasty, just as I am building mine."

"We all made sacrifices back then. Some of us benefited more from them than others," she said, lowering her gaze. Lazarus felt the bite of long-ago as rooted rage shot through his limbs. Images of burning buildings and mad laughter echoing in memories forged at the beginning of his life.

"Don't tell me about sacrifices—"

"Then I suggest you don't insult me again by presuming to declare debts owed. We are both self-made people, Lazarus. There is little doubt that even without the alliance of my people, you will likely survive."

"I want assurances, Imogen," Lazarus replied. "Why do you deny me?" He sat forward. Almost as readily, she sat back. The mouse to his cat despite her own preference for playing the clawed creature. "An alliance between Norcasta and Ilvas can bring nothing but fortune," he continued. "Through me, you will be protected. The Ciseans will be required to honor my peace with you. And in forming a treaty with the N'skari, the same rules will apply."

The Queen remained quiet for a moment, tapping her fingers against her thigh as she considered his words. Closing her eyes, Imogen leaned her head back. "I recall when you were just a boy. Barely a man . . ." she trailed off with a shake of her head. "No, you've always been a man in my mind. Your body has simply caught up. You always were a perfect specimen of lethal resolve. You don't need me."

"The alliance, Imogen," Lazarus said, not fettered by her pretty words as he brought them back to the issue at hand. "You must agree to it." When she still didn't answer him, choosing instead to suck another drag from her pipe, Lazarus leaned forward further. His arms rested on his knees as he spoke the words guaranteed to make the woman across from him reconsider her refusal. "You know what he is capable of, Imogen. He's already sent one person into your court without your knowing. Do you truly want to be without allies if he ever decides to leave his corner of the world?"

She paused, her hand quivering slightly as she reached for the pipe again. The tips of her fingers had turned a shade bluer. Her lips were pale, and her expression drawn.

"He has no reason to venture north—"

"He has no reason for many of the things he has done, but he still does them. Would you like to gamble with the lives of your people, yourself—

your daughter—gamble that he won't come for you when he decides he's grown bored of his own court's games? When he tires of merely meddling in our affairs?"

Closing her eyes against the implied warning Lazarus gave her, the Pirate Queen's demeanor grew rock hard; from the tension in her body to the stony expression of her face. And then . . . it all dropped away. Shoulders releasing and drooping, eyes drifting open, Imogen met Lazarus' gaze, and in the depths of her eyes, he saw resignation.

"A lot has happened these last few days," she said with a sigh. "You've proven yourself intelligent, and if not honorable, then at least loyal to your own. Your vassals have done far more than that."

"Imogen," he said, growing impatient by her evasions though he knew she recognized that he was right. "As the next heir of Norcasta, will you form an alliance with me?"

Imogen reached for the pipe again and took a long drag. "I have stipulations," she eventually.

He didn't move. "Name them."

"There's to be a bridge of honesty and open trade between our kingdoms. Ilvan merchants are to be given priority in the capital of Leone and protected rights against the slave trade. I've had too many men and women taken under Claudius' reign and sold as property. He would not take action against his lords. You must."

"Done," Lazarus agreed readily.

"If and when the N'skari are brought in, there will be discussions had about my ships that are continuously sunk near their waters. I want plans in place to prevent further encounters."

He wanted to ask why she was sailing so close to N'skari waters, but that was a conversation to be had when his alliance with them was actually achieved. "We'll discuss it when the time comes. I cannot promise reparations, but a compromise can be met." She nodded once. "Is there anything else?"

"I'll want someone I can trust without reserve in your court," she said. "As intriguing as your white raksasa is, she is—unequivocally—*yours*. I'm afraid her loyalty is unquestionable. I need the same."

"You shall have it," Lazarus assured her.

"Axe will travel with you to N'skara." Lazarus opened his mouth, but she continued speaking. "In return, I will gift you and your house with an Ilvan ship of the highest quality, and a crew to sail you there. My ships are fast and durable. You will reach your destinations with no trouble. In return, I would—"

"Your Highness," Lazarus interrupted. "As understandable as it is to want someone trustworthy in my court, your daughter is too young for such a thing."

Imogen looked down her nose at him before leaning forward and taking up her pipe, putting the end to her lips. She inhaled and sighed. "This is non-negotiable, Lord Fierté," she said. "If you take issue and wish to leave someone with me . . ." she trailed off, letting her meaning hang between them.

Lazarus shook his head. "I require the use of all of my current vassals."

She nodded. "I understand. If you change your mind later, I'll receive whomever you send with open arms. Axe will be overjoyed at this opportunity."

"I will agree to take someone of your house with me—I've done the same with Thorne. But as your heir, don't you think your daughter should remain with you?"

Imogen's shoulders lifted and then slowly descended as she released a long stream of smoke into the air above their heads. "What my daughter needs is to be unrestrained," she replied. "Here, she is happy, but I can see the longing in her eyes every time she looks out at the bay. She has a burning desire for adventure. I had my opportunity for adventure at her age. It would be remiss of me to bind her here and deprive her of the chance." The Pirate Queen looked down her pipe at Lazarus with lowered brows. "I'm sure you understand the necessity of giving our closest companions the power to choose for themselves where they will go."

Lazarus did not have a response for that. The most immediate answer came to him in the image of Quinn's face, focused and full of dark pride. She was as untamable as the ocean, as unpredictable as a storm. Just as Imogen wanted to give Axe the chance to break free from her bonds, Lazarus wanted to see what Quinn could do were she to be released as well.

"Alright," Lazarus agreed with an edge of resignation. "I accept."

Imogen grinned and nodded in approval. "Spoken like a true king."

"I'd like to leave tomorrow," he said.

"That can be arranged." Reaching up, Imogen tugged on a long rope dangling from the ceiling near her chaise. As a servant came hurrying into the room to appease whatever the Queen desired, Lazarus stood to leave. "It was a pleasure speaking with you, Lord Fierté," the Queen called.

"And you, Your Highness." He bowed low and then exited as Imogen began barking orders at the servant to fetch her captain of the guard. By this time tomorrow, he would be well on his way to the brutally cold land that was N'skara.

Voyage to Winter

"The past is a dangerous thing, because eventually it will catch up to the present."
— Quinn Darkova, vassal of House Fierté, fear twister, white raksasa

Quinn sidled over the wet planks and leaned forward, resting her forearms against the railing. The wind whipped, flinging strands of lavender across her face. She brushed them away with a flick of her wrist and looked to the docks down below, where Lazarus finished directing the last of their crew. Men and women, primarily ex-pirates, that he'd had to debrief on where they were going and what they would be doing. If all went well, this would be a short sailing excursion and they'd be home to their families and homeland in a few weeks.

If it didn't go well . . . they wouldn't be coming home.

Quinn wondered briefly if the crew knew what she was—and if they did, would they still be risking themselves. If they would still set off on this perilous voyage, sleeping and working alongside someone as dangerous as her, heading to one of the most treacherous places in the world.

N'skara was as cold and unforgiving as its people.

Her people.

Quinn shook her head, clearing away the melancholic thoughts as the last of the crew loaded up. Lazarus turned, catching her gaze. His black eyes reflecting that darkness in him. He clenched his fists, and she caught a hint of the souls beneath his tunic as their essence peeked around his cuff, the dark markings drawing her attention. Her eyes dropped to it before rising back to his. She raised an eyebrow, and he scowled, pulling the cuff of his sleeve down.

She smirked at that.

"Imogen," Lazarus said, turning to look down the docks. Quinn followed his line of sight and saw the Queen and her red-haired child strolling toward them. She wore dark leather pants and a fine woven shirt that was a tad loose for her slender frame. She tossed her long, dark braid over her shoulder and smiled in greeting.

"Lazarus," she replied in kind.

Quinn blinked. *Since when are they so informal?* Her smirk slowly subsided as her eyes slid over to Axe, who was dressed in thick trousers and carried a cloak of fur. A leather bag hung from her side, and Quinn had the good sense to recognize a complication when she saw it.

When Imogen came to a stop before Lazarus, but Axe kept walking, climbing the plank—that suspicion turned into dread. Her attention shot back to Lazarus, and she narrowed her eyes.

She turned her hand, pulling on that whisper of fear that everyone had. He whipped around and glared back at her. "What in the dark realm are you thinking?" she hissed, just low enough she'd hoped the girl wouldn't notice.

"I'm *Madara's* emissary, just as Vaughn is the Cisean's," Axe replied. Quinn pursed her lips, tilting her head.

"I hope that you will take good care of my daughter on your journey, Quinn," the Queen said. There was enough of an edge to her voice that foretold of what exactly would happen should she fail to do so, but Quinn didn't fear her idled threats— she only felt annoyance toward the unwanted addition to their group. Quinn bit the inside of her cheek and stared down at the Pirate Queen.

"I'll take such good care of her, the urchin will wish she'd never left home," she answered. Imogen laughed softly and nodded once before placing a hand on Lazarus' shoulder and turning him away. They spoke in hushed voices, and if Axe could just walk a little bit quieter, she might be able to hear—

"I have somethin' for you," the young woman's voice squawked beside her. Quinn turned brittle in her movements as she glanced over her shoulder. Axe pulled her satchel forward and opened the top.

Despite her frustrations, Quinn's curiosity got the better of her, and she found herself leaning forward. "What is it?" she asked.

Axe reached in and pulled out something metal that gleamed gold in the sunlight.

"Within pirates, loyalty isn't always guaranteed, because it can be bought. When one does a favor for another, it's traditional to either pay them, or owe them a debt," Axe started as she pulled a second item from the bag, also with a gold sheen. Quinn eyed it with interest. "You captured the traitor in her court."

"I take it she'd prefer to pay me rather than owe me," she remarked.

"Aye, that would be *Madara's* way." Axe extended both her closed fists and turned them over, opening her fingers.

"Are those—" Quinn reached forward, grasping one between her fingers.

"Brass knuckles, but she had them plated in gold," Axe answered. "She thought you'd prefer them over jewelry." Quinn turned the weapon in her hand and eyed a familiar symbol.

A snake with its mouth open and fangs extended wove through a crowned skull, curved horns protruding from the white bone. Wings spanned behind it; the hilt of a sword peeked above the ornate diadem. It was Lazarus' crest. The one she wore upon her tunic to signify the house she served. In every spare section of the metal, rubies had been inlaid. Quinn gripped the brass knuckles in one hand and took the other from Axe.

"I do," she answered solemnly. "Thank you."

Axe scrunched her nose. "I'm not the one you

should be thanking. As far as I'm concerned, you're still a hussy." With that, she turned on her heel and strode below deck with only a wave in her mother's direction. The Pirate Queen waved back and then turned her eyes to Quinn. The warning she'd given her was still clear, but Quinn was beginning to think these weren't just for Zorel. They were for the journey to come.

Imogen had gifted her with a weapon; one expensive enough should she ever leave this house, it would buy her a good life. Quinn didn't know how to express thanks well, but she knew how to show understanding. She looked to Axe, and then back to the Queen and nodded once.

Imogen smiled, and it had nothing to do with whatever Lazarus was saying.

Quinn turned away from them and faced the sea. The waves were oddly peaceful this morning. The sun was shining, and she soaked up its warmth knowing that where they were going there would be no such feeling. Only a cold so bitter that it burned.

Heavy footsteps pounded behind her, and the loading ramp came up. Shouts sounded as the crew leapt into action and the ship began moving. Quinn leaned onto the railing, inhaling deeply.

"What'd she give you?" Lazarus asked. Quinn

silently extended the brass knuckles, and he took one, examining its gold curves and jeweled embellishments. "If I didn't know better, I'd say she was trying to buy you." Out of the corner of her eye, Quinn saw him brush his thumb over the crest.

"It's payment," she answered as the sails unfurled. A gust of wind hit them, and they started to gain speed.

"For Zorel?"

"Among other things," Quinn answered. They shared a look, and he nodded slowly, placing it back in her hand. She curled her fingers around it, stowing them both in her pocket.

"It'll be a nice addition with the staff you took from Siva," he said, gripping the railing when the first real wave hit them, and the ship bobbed.

Quinn smirked. "I won that staff," she answered, fingering the wooden length that hung from her side.

"Mhmm," he murmured. "It makes me wonder what you'll be bringing back from N'skara."

Quinn froze, if only for a second. He didn't know. He couldn't. Not *yet*.

"Nothing," she answered, harsher than intended. Her lips pressed together as she turned her head away.

"Nothing?" he asked. She could tell he was prying now.

"Lazarus, did it ever occur to you that there was a reason I left?" Quinn kept her voice nonchalant as she turned from the railing. She could feel his eyes on her back as she started for her cabin.

They heard a screech so loud it forced her to look overhead.

A black bird flew in the direction they were going, but on an errant wind of cold that defied the warmth of Tritol, and a single feather drifted in front of her.

Silver.

Not black.

Quinn swallowed as it came to land on her outstretched hand. She curled her fingers around it and shook her head once before she kept walking. Lazarus wasn't completely wrong, just as she wasn't being completely honest.

The question wasn't *what* she was bringing back from N'skara.

It was *who*.

A Trade in Secrets

"Some trade in gold, and others time, but for those that know the darker facets of life—it is secrets that truly have worth beyond measure."
— *Quinn Darkova, vassal of House Fierté, fear twister, white raksasa*

Waves pounded against the hull, gently rocking the ship. The wooden cup of water on the nightstand rattled, and Quinn's hand shot out. Black tendrils jumped from her fingertips just as it started to tilt sideways. The cup landed on the nightstand, and Quinn sighed, pulling back her magic.

"You've gotten better," Lorraine croaked. Her voice was as cracked as her lips, but she was on the mend. Slowly, but surely.

"I've been practicing," Quinn replied, patting her face with a dry cloth. The fever had broken, but she wasn't back to full strength just yet.

"I can tell," she answered. There was a contentedness in her face as she watched Quinn move around her, checking her bandage and adjusting it as she instructed. Once Lorraine had been tended to, Quinn sat back and wiped the perspiration from her own brow. Being below deck was becoming more stifling the longer she stayed there, but Quinn continued to sweat it out in order to help Lorraine recover as quickly as possible.

That was one casualty she did not want to be responsible for when they got to N'skara.

"Alright, I think you're set. Is there anything else I can help with?" she asked. The sly smile on Lorraine's face made her falter.

"My, my, who would have thought you had manners in you after all?"

Quinn sucked in a breath, and Lorraine doubled over, a grating chuckle sliding from her lips. She laughed twice before it turned into a cough, a groan ending her chortle. Quinn stood there dumbstruck while she settled back, still oddly amused for someone bedbound and confined to the cabin.

"Are you sure—" she started.

"I'm fine," Lorraine answered, before she could say anything more. "Send Dominicus down if you see him." With one hand, she shooed Quinn toward the door, and while she couldn't make her do anything, Quinn backed away with both hands raised.

"I just don't want a repeat of you almost dying while I'm here," she grumbled, turning to appraise the man that just entered the room silently.

Dominicus' apathetic gaze swept over her before he nodded once and stepped out of her way. It seemed that while he hadn't forgiven her for leaving out the details about the healer poisoning Lorraine, he did appreciate her finding the real threat, and by happenstance, getting them out of there, with a ship no less. He hadn't said a word about their visits, nor would he, so long as Lorraine remained safe when Quinn was there.

She nodded her chin once in return before retreating down the hallway. The door closed behind her as she reached the steps that would take her up. Quinn sighed and took them two at a time, her head popping out into the open air right as an axe went careening by—missing her face by mere inches.

"What in the dark realm!" she yelled, her eyebrows lowering as she tilted her head back to look where the axe had just been—and to the reckless child that threw it. Axe stood over a collapsed Vaughn, cackling madly with her hand in the air—and magically, the weapon returned to her.

Quinn huffed a breath, striding forward, black wisps gathered at her fingertips as she narrowed her eyes on the girl. Axe's laugh died out, and she wiped the water from her eyes, extending a hand toward Vaughn.

Lazarus' warm fingers wrapped around her bare forearm, pulling her to a stop. Quinn froze.

"I thought we'd come to an understanding about you harming my other vassals."

"She's not *yours*," Quinn answered icily. "Therefore—"

"She's an emissary, and I promised her mother. Furthermore, so did you." The tone of his voice made her shiver, and she glanced to his hand, still clutching her arm. His nails gripped her tight, biting into the flesh. The piercing jolt stirred things in her—darker, far more wicked things. Nothing like what she considered doing to Axe.

"Is that all?" she asked him softly, leaning into his touch. She held her ground as the moment suspended between them, waiting to see what he would do. Waiting for him.

"Oy!" a shout rang out. "You can't do that— what are—you backwards talkin', troll walkin' brute!" Axe's voice acted as a blade, cutting through whatever was brewing between Quinn and Lazarus. He clenched his jaw, the muscle twitching as he released her.

She pulled away and sighed, and that only seemed to inflame his agitation more. Ire flashed through his expression, and Lazarus stepped back. "We're not done here."

Quinn quirked an eyebrow, crossing her arms over her chest. "We're not?"

Lazarus tugged at one of his sleeves. A flinty tenor entered his voice as he said, "No. You've been keeping secrets, and I'm quite sure you have more. I'd like to find out what they are and why."

They stared at each other a moment more, Axe hollering in the background, when Quinn said, "Goodluck with that, *Prince*. Perhaps Fortuna will smile upon you yet."

She knew that it wasn't smart to rile him up, nor was it in her best interest to encourage his questioning—certainly not when they were heading into N'skara—but she couldn't help herself. Quinn flashed him a taunting grin and turned on her heel, leaving Lazarus staring after her.

Across from her, Vaughn stood holding Axe upside down by her ankles. The little urchin was cursing him, using every word in Ilvan and Norcastan, and when those ran out, she switched to something else. A language Quinn had never heard before. The mountain man didn't seem too perturbed by her words as he continued shaking her. Something slipped free of her trouser pocket and hit the wooden planks with a thump.

Vaughn paused, peering over the ends of her boots. He shook his head, laying her down as gently as could be expected before picking up the object. Quinn squinted, looking between the two of them.

"Is that your hunting knife?" Quinn asked, glancing at the sharpened stone he held and then to Axe's pockets where it had been. "What was it doing in her possession?" She narrowed her eyes on the younger girl, some of her earlier annoyance returning.

"Little pirate was practicing," Vaughn said, stowing the knife in his sheath at his hip.

"Mhmm," Quinn hummed. "Practicing?"

"Vaughn okay, she-wolf Quinn. No need to kill little pirate, yes?"

She wasn't sure she bought the whole "practicing" nonsense, but Quinn had no true intentions of hurting the girl. Much as she might annoy her at times, Lazarus was right, at least in that. She couldn't harm her any more than she could any of his other vassals, per the terms of their contract. She also wasn't in a hurry to give back the brass knuckles she'd been given by Imogen for keeping the urchin out of trouble.

Quinn was only just beginning to understand how hard that might be on a ship setting sail for the infernal cold, with no one but ex-pirates and her own comrades for company, and nothing else to see but the big blue. She brushed her palm over her jaw, swiping her thumb across her bottom lip.

"No kill?" Vaughn asked again.

Quinn rolled her eyes. "I'm not going to kill her, Vaughn. I'd never hear the end of it."

At that, the *little pirate* decided to pipe up. "Oy! You think I can't take you, hussy——"

"She-wolf Quinn is fierce," Vaughn said, interrupting the girl. He leveled her with a look of authority. "It is unwise to provoke her."

Axe narrowed her eyes at him. "Pfft," she muttered, blowing a sweaty lock of hair from her face. Quinn shook her head and sighed.

"You," she motioned to the girl. Axe scrunched her nose. "Come with me."

"Why?"

Quinn didn't answer as she started for the bow of the ship, to the very front point where it was only ocean and sky in every direction. She leaned forward, resting her weight against the railing as another form sidled up beside her. Axe mimicked her motions, leaning forward and stealing glances when she thought Quinn wasn't watching.

"How much do you know about the N'skari?" she asked her eventually.

Axe blew out an exaggerated heavy breath. "Not much. They all look like you. They don't drink or smoke. They speak like they're better than the rest of us." The young woman shrugged. "Why?" she asked again. She liked that word, Quinn noticed. She enjoyed prying, stealing; marauding through people's secrets, and while she gave reckless a new meaning, she was also uncharacteristically observant.

"Because that's where we're going, and no one on this ship realizes how poorly this could end for you all with just a single word," Quinn replied, intentionally vague. Axe looked over at her, her auburn eyebrows drawn together.

"That sounds ominous."

"That's because it is," she said. "In N'skara, the smallest infractions are dealt with severe punishments. Were you to try that stunt you did with Vaughn, you'd be lucky if they only cut off both your hands. Being an outsider, they're far more likely to just kill you."

Axe shivered, and Quinn thought she might be starting to get it. This wasn't just an adventure. It wasn't simply dangerous. For a girl like Axe, N'skara could spell her death if she didn't learn to tread carefully.

"That's . . . harsh," Axe said eventually.

"It's their way of life. The way they've always been. The way they will always be." Images surfaced from the depths of her mind; flashes of silver hair and flint-colored skin. She heard peals of laughter in the distance, followed by screams and sounds of fear—so much fear that it suffocated. Blood stained her past, present, and if she had her way—future.

"Is that why you left?" Axe asked, pulling her from those dark places. She'd closed herself off to the memories years ago. It wasn't a surprise that they were choosing to now surface when she was so close to carrying out her final plan. Her last act that would set her free.

"I . . ." Quinn hesitated, considering how to phrase her answer. "I never fit in. My family were mostly white Maji, and I was born about as dark as one can be. Growing up was difficult because I longed to embrace what I was, but at every turn, I was told I was wrong. Twisted." Now when she thought of those words, they held a new meaning. Instead of the barrier they had been, they'd became her mantra. *Twisted*. She had always been this way —and just as set in her ways as her people, she always would be.

"I can understand that," Axe said softly. Quinn frowned slightly, tilting her head a fraction. "I'm Imogen's daughter and hold claim to a throne that some people believe I don't deserve."

"Because you're not of her blood?" Quinn asked. "You know, Lazarus isn't of King Claudius' blood either, and he's taking the throne. At least you don't have other heirs to contend with."

"That's only part of it." Axe sighed, and that

heaviness that she'd seen the night Imogen was poisoned resurfaced. "I'm not her blood, but I'm not even blood to anyone on this continent." Quinn turned her head a little more, the corner of one eyebrow starting to go up.

"You were an orphan. That's—"

"Do you know how Imogen found me?" Axe interrupted.

Quinn paused. "No, I can't say I do."

The young girl smiled, but it didn't reach her eyes. The corners were too strained. The sadness in her eyes too deep to hide with humor. "Don't you find it interestin' that while most of the continent knows that I exist, no one knows where or how *Madara* found me?"

Quinn's lips parted. "If you don't come from the Sirian continent . . ."

Axe looked over, and there was knowledge there. Secrets. Above all else, there was a darkness, not like that of Quinn or Lazarus, but one that was caused rather than formed on its own. One that haunted her—like Draeven.

"If you tell me why you left N'skara, I'll tell you my story," Axe said. Quinn narrowed her eyes a fraction, looking for how she was attempting to exploit the answers given, but Axe wasn't manipulating. The bargain was clear. A secret for a secret. A trade.

"Alright," Quinn said. They were going to find out her reasons for ending up in Norcasta soon enough anyways. "Let's hear it."

Axe unclipped the canteen at her belt. She flipped open the top and took a swig of something that smelled suspiciously like plum liquor.

"I came from a village on the coast. My parents were farmers, but before that, they'd been soldiers. I had two brothers, but it's been so long I can hardly remember what they looked like. I only know their names," Axe started. "It's funny how time does that, you know?" The young woman shook her head, as if trying to clear those thoughts away. "I can still remember the day it happened. I was sittin' on the roof when the fires started. One minute, the skies were clear, and the next, black clouds were rollin' in. The air smelled of smoke and burnin' flesh." Axe's fingers gripped the railing so tight her knuckles had turned white.

"What happened?" Quinn asked, eyeing the girl beside her reproachfully.

"Soldiers," Axe answered. "The famine had gone on too long and people blamed the farmers. They swept through, seizin' land and killin' people.

Cookin' them while they were at it." The way she spoke was detached; as if she saw the memory but existed outside of it. Quinn could understand that sort of apathy. "I was told to hide in the closet, but then they came to our house and they were lookin' for somethin'. I watched . . ." She trailed off, swallowing hard. "Bad things. They did real bad things to my parents, but when they turned to my brothers, I couldn't stop myself." Quinn frowned, but Axe continued on without missing a beat. "I killed them. The four that were there. I don't know how. I shouldn't have been able to; a little girl and four men the size of that green-eyed git." She threw a dirty look over her shoulder at Vaughn before turning back. Somberness took hold. "But I took a hatchet to every single one of them." Axe took another swig of her liquor, and Quinn wondered if she needed it for this. "It didn't save my brothers . . . the guards killed them as soon as I took out the first one. I don't know how long passed after that—I just stood there in that house covered in their blood."

"Imogen found you after that?" Quinn asked.

"No," Axe sighed. "Not yet. After that, I ran for days. I don't know how many. I ran until I collapsed, slept it off, and ran again. I don't remember how I made it through those first days. But one morning, I woke up on a beach, and a woman was there. She was Saltira."

"The goddess of war?" Quinn asked, skepticism entering her voice.

Axe nodded. "She took my hatchet and gave me these in return. They were gifts, for my bravery."

"How did you know she was a goddess?"

"Well, for starters, she told me."

Quinn gave her a deadpanned look and pursed her lips. "And you believe everything people tell you?"

Axe chuckled. "I can see magic."

"And . . ." Quinn prompted, still perplexed.

"She was *made* of it." Axe shrugged. "You Maji control it, but most of you don't have it *inside* you. Saltira looked like she was made of fire, it was so bright."

"Uh huh . . ." Quinn said, not entirely sure if she believed it, but she couldn't deny what she had seen. The axes did things that could only be explained by magic.

"She told me that I was the daughter of her heart, but I was of this world and the 'mother of my soul' would find me. I just had to stay on the beach. So, I listened. And three days later, *Madara* came."

Quinn leaned back, blowing out a breath. "And where exactly did she come?"

In a smaller voice, almost a whisper, Axe answered, "The Crystal Continent." Quinn turned that over in her mind, not sure how much was true and how much was the distorted memories of a child. "*Madara* found me clutching these," she said, holding out one of her weapons. "I didn't know Ilvan yet, but she named me Axelle that day. Axe for short, and I've gone by it ever since."

"You know," Quinn started. "That's crazy enough most people probably wouldn't believe it."

Axe laughed once. "Some of the crew that were there that day took issue with me being named heir. When they tried to stir up a rebellion, *Madara* made them disappear, and with them, my story. No one but my family—and now you—know where I come from." She squinted sideways at Quinn for a second. "So, if you blab, I'll know where to throw this next."

Quinn snorted. "Lazarus is currently allied with your mother. I wouldn't concern yourself too much."

"So," Axe started. "I told you my story. Why'd you leave N'skara?"

Quinn smiled because the answer was as simple as it was complicated.

"I didn't simply leave. I was sold."

Like cattle, by a family that valued their secrets more than their blood. Quinn didn't share those thoughts, not even when Axe started rattling off questions.

"By who? How? I was told they didn't support slavery."

"They don't," Quinn replied. *Not officially.*

"But then—how? What happened?" Axe asked, and Quinn merely smiled.

"I told you why I left. That was the terms of our agreement, little pirate. Perhaps you should spend more time practicing negotiation instead of pilfering things that don't belong to you. Hmm?" She grinned, and Axe's mouth fell open for a brief moment.

"Black Baac," she snapped, recovering. "You know that's not what I meant when I—"

"But it's what you *said*," Quinn interrupted. "Maybe take this as a lesson and consider what I've told you. We'll be in N'skara in a few days, and if you try this with one of them, you'll wind up sacrificed to some god. *Savvy?*"

She walked away, whistling to herself the sailor's song she'd heard morning and night in those early days when her wrists had been bound and she'd been stored in the cargo hold of a ship. Trapped. Caged. Those memories didn't eat her alive anymore, because she took them. She used them, and she let herself become the monster they thought her to be.

And now, she was coming home.

She was coming for retribution.

A Game of Truths

"There are no absolutes in life. Even truths can change based on a differing perspective."
— *Lazarus Fierté, soul eater, heir to Norcasta, frustrated prince*

L eviathan's eye hovered high in the midnight sky. Dark water rose and fell around them, pushing them further toward the cold wasteland he sought. The night crew moved about quietly, but not so quiet as the woman standing at the bow. She stood leaning forward just so, her forearms pressed against the railing for support. Her hands were together, fingers interwoven and unmoving even as a spritz of sea water slapped her across the chest. She didn't look down, nor did she brush the icy droplets away. Her gaze stayed locked on something far in the distance that none of them could see.

Lazarus moved forward from the shadows to join her. The white blouse she wore was a mere wisp of cloth when water soaked the front portion and the wind whipped it tightly around her frame. Lazarus' eyes didn't stray lower than her neckline, for those were thoughts for another time.

"Axe doesn't know how to play the game just yet," he started. If she was surprised by his presence, she didn't show it.

"No," Quinn said. "But she thinks she does, and that's even more dangerous among the wrong people."

"Is that how you learned?" he asked her, resting an arm against the railing. He leaned into it with his side, facing her entirely.

"I don't think it's been a week just yet," she answered evasively.

"I don't particularly care," Lazarus replied. "You're keeping secrets that affect this house; that without me knowing can hurt this house."

She responded with a slight upturn of her lips.

"I was wondering when we would be back to this," she said.

"I made it clear how I felt about you keeping se—"

"You have the audacity to scold me about keeping secrets when you've never been forth-coming with your own?" A harder edge entered her tone, one that made him think she wasn't in the mood to play the game tonight. He pushed forward.

"I am the master—"

"You are a lord and a dark Maji," she snapped back, still not looking at him. "One day you might even be king—but you do not own me." Lazarus clenched his jaw, gritting his teeth.

"The fact of the matter remains that I am the one in charge. You are my vassal. You work for me. I tell you things when you need to know them, the same as every other vassal—"

"That's a lie."

Lazarus leaned back. "What did you say?"

"I said," Quinn turned, facing him finally, "that's a lie. You tell us things when you deem it worth our notice, but it's not when or what we necessarily need to know. The same as I do for you, because while I might work for you, you do not own me. No one does, nor will anyone ever again." Her pale skin was ethereal under the moonlight. It seemed to shimmer and glow, almost soft if not for the hardness of her jaw or darkness in her gaze. Her lavender hair looked a deep shade of gray in the night. Were it not for the anger in her expression, she might have been too unblemished to be real. Instead, she mimicked a colorless stone no different than those of the gods this world loved to worship. Not even Saltira, the goddess of war, could imitate such ruthlessness in a single expression.

"I don't know what you think you have learned, but I tell you things when you need to know them. If I thought it—"

"How did you get the scar on your face?" she asked.

Lazarus stopped, and despite the chill, his blood warmed. It burned. He knew where this was going. When she'd turned and looked at him while questioning Zorel, it wasn't for guidance or anything else. It was because she recognized the scar on his face.

Lazarus had the same one.

"You don't need to know that," Lazarus said curtly. She raised an eyebrow, questioning him. Always questioning him.

"I don't need to know that, you say." She leaned

forward, lowering her voice to a whisper. "But the man I saw in Zorel's mind was the same man that attacked us on the road. He's the man that framed me—and he has a scar the same as yours." A fog was rolling in over the sea, and it froze the hair on his face with its bite. Beneath the cold air and frigid water was this mass inside his chest that was blackened and bloody and raw.

He'd left the past behind him.

He'd moved forward into a new age.

Yet, here Quinn stood, asking questions she shouldn't know to ask.

Lazarus leaned forward, and their breaths mingled. "Listen to me and listen closely. Whatever you saw—whomever you saw—he's not your problem right now. I am." She didn't even blink, and he wondered when it was that his warnings stopped fazing her . . . or if they ever did in the first place. "And I don't look kindly on vassals that lie to me. You knew how to speak Ilvan, but you kept that from me. You went after an assassin sent for the Queen—a mission that if you had failed would've likely earned you a stone tied to your neck and your body cast in the bay. A dead vassal is a useless vassal."

She grinned like he'd complimented her instead

of reprimanded, and Lazarus cursed himself. *How did I fall so far from power when it comes to her?* He asked himself this question daily, and still, he did not have an answer.

"I suppose it's a good thing that I'm not useless, then, isn't it?" she asked, smirking to herself. "Good that I can not only break out of jail, but can find and retrieve the correct man, make him confess before Imogen, and get you your alliance." She turned her head a fraction, letting her eyes sweep over the mast and the sails, glancing at the helm and over the deck. "As well as all of this. You have plenty of use for me. Don't talk at me about vassals who are *useless*." She spat the word with a cruel smile on her lips, and the heat in his chest flared, his groin stiffening.

"You need to be more honest with me and stop keeping secrets," he reiterated.

"You should trust me a little more and be worthy of that honesty," she shot back. Her gaze was strong as steel, her posture stiff as the wood planks he stood on. "You need me, and you can't deny that. I don't know how you've gained an audience in N'skara, but without me, you'll achieve nothing. Everyone is useless there *except* me."

Lazarus sighed and nodded, unable to refute

her worth when they arrived in her homeland. "Yes, you will be crucial in gaining an audience—"

Quinn paused, the smile dropping into a firm line. "Will be?" she said. "Do you mean to tell me you haven't gained an audience?"

He paused, taking in her flat tone of voice. An inkling of dread settled in his stomach as he slowly said, "I sent a letter informing them of our arrival and my wish to speak with them, the same as I had with Thorne and Imogen. We left Shallowyn ahead of schedule, and we were well into the Cisean mountains before a response would have come." Quinn gaped at him.

"You sent a letter? That's it?" Her eyes widened, anger flashing as she spoke. "What were you thinking? Do you wish to kill us all? The N'skari don't allow outsiders without invitation. Even trader ships need invitation before entering the waters of N'skara. You are a fool, Lazarus Fierté," she hissed. "They will not welcome you because of your noble blood or your status as heir—"

"I am noble by right, not by blood; understand that," he interrupted her. "I'll request an audience upon greeting the council."

"None of that matters to the N'skari," Quinn countered. "You should have told me. You should have answered my questions when I asked them." She sighed deeply, the annoyance she felt permeating the air.

"As you should have answered mine," Lazarus said through gritted teeth.

"Sometimes you have to give before you get," she snapped back. Silence formed between them, broken only by the choppy waters and the blood in his ears.

"Very well. You've made your point," he said eventually. "A question for a question, then. I'll give you an answer as good as I get." He lifted a brow. "Agreed?"

Quinn looked over his face, her attention pausing on his lips. She inhaled once and exhaled the damning scent of hers. *Damp petals and fresh snow,* he thought, inhaling greedily. She didn't smell like lilacs or vanilla, as many women chose to. She smelled like she tasted—of dark magic and darker desires.

She leaned away, and the souls beneath his skin vied for power. They sought her out like a bloodlion on a scent. Something about her drew them, and she knew it.

Quinn nodded once, her gaze skimming down over his cuffs before coming back up. "Ask your question, Dark Prince, and perhaps you'll be smarter than the girl about it."

Lazarus wasn't sure whether he should smirk or grimace, and he settled for watching her. "I would ask what else you're keeping from me, but I suspect the list is longer of what you are than what you aren't." She snorted once and looked back out over the waves, but she didn't say he was wrong. "So instead, I'll ask another one. Where did you learn and how did they teach you to play this game we do?"

"That's two questions in one," Quinn said. "But I'll answer them anyways." He could tell in that moment that whatever she was seeing in the distance, it was not the waves. "I learned to play as a child in N'skara, but it was leaving that taught me to play as I do. No one is as great a teacher as time."

"You didn't answer how," he pointed out.

"How does anyone learn?" She looked back at him. "By losing. Nothing is as great a motivator as fear."

"You can fear?" he asked, expecting her not to answer.

"As you have a soul. Like calls to like, Lazarus, and in some ways, you and I are the same."

The hairs along his neck prickled in anticipation. "Ask me your question, Quinn."

She didn't. Not at first. He knew she was toying with him when whole minutes passed before she finally gave him her attention again.

When she did ask, it was not the question he expected. It was worse.

"Who gave you that scar?"

Lazarus blanched before answering. He promised her the truth, and he delivered it.

"Someone who was once a friend," he said. She didn't ask for a name. He didn't feel obliged to give it.

"But not anymore?" she mused.

"You asked your question, and I gave you an answer. Just because you answered multiple inquiries doesn't mean I will." Instead of looking irritated, she seemed content. Pleased by his response. It unsettled him.

"You look bothered," she noted.

"You didn't respond as I expected you to. I've learned that when that happens with you, I should be wary." Quinn laughed lightly, and it danced on the wind.

"Much like Axe, you think you know more than

you do," she replied. "I learn as much from what you don't say as what you do."

Lazarus' lips parted, but he didn't say anything. Turning on his heel, he left her at the bow and returned to his cabin. As he readied for bed and well into the night, all he could think about was what she said.

And what she didn't.

The Fallen Temple

"Even as we humans forget, the gods will not."
— *Quinn Darkova, vassal of House Fierté, fear twister,*
white raksasa

G*lass cracked beneath her feet, each shard cutting deep into her flesh until it was lodged inside, making every step forward more painful. The broken bits jutted upward from the ground, a spike next to each sparse blade of grass—as though they were growing there naturally, side by side. Quinn's blood stained the sharp edges as she passed over them.*

She focused her eyes forward, taking in the strangeness of a land she recognized. The impoverished buildings were familiar to her; the box-like structures with their paper-thin outer walls and sloped roofs hanging over the open doorways. Each was built to withstand the harsh winds of a blizzard, the framework solid despite the thin layer of covering that cloaked the sides of the humble dwellings. Yet inside, Quinn knew there would still be a hearth to create a fire for warmth on the coldest of nights.

Why?

Because N'skara was different. Its people were different. Its very climate was unnatural. The wind may have whipped and beaten, the snow may have fallen—unforgiving and never ceasing—but it was all for the sake of remaining unseen and untouched. N'skara was a wasteland of magic. Close enough to the dark realm to instill fear, far enough from the rest of the world to encourage ignorance.

Quinn's feet left the grass as she neared the edge of a street, and the glass-coated soil was replaced by ice-cold cobblestones. The pain in her feet receded, leaving room for the feeling of nostalgia—and grotesque hatred began to rise up.

As she strode down the pathway, Quinn's eyes trailed to either side, observing the hanging of textiles in the doorways and the wooden charms meant to ward off Mazzulah's creatures of the dark. She scowled. The N'skari were a bunch of superstitious fools. And yet, she was a part of them. She was born N'skari. She used to walk these streets as a child. She wore the same colorless robes as the other *nobles. But a pure, white cloth could never cover what she was in this place.*

Unwelcome.

Twisted.

Dark.

A shadowed figure swooped across her line of sight, drawing Quinn's attention. She came to a slow halt as black and silver feathers fluttered overhead, and a single plume drifted to the ground at her feet. It was the bird—not just any bird—but the one she'd seen before. The creature circled just above her head, rounding once, twice, three times before flitting away, straight down the street.

Quinn's fists tightened, but she hurried after it, nonetheless. The animal picked up a burst of speed, its wings spreading wide and whipping sideways as it veered down one street and then the next. Sweat broke out across her forehead and a few beads rolled down the back of her neck as she struggled to keep up with it. Her thighs began to burn, the soles of her feet ached as they pounded on the uneven stones, making every glass shard dig deeper into her skin. Every once in a while, Quinn would turn her head, looking for an N'skari, but no one emerged from the dwellings.

She was alone.

Well, perhaps not truly alone, *Quinn thought as she refocused upon the winged creature above her, leading her through the maze of buildings.*

The bird would slow its speed every so often, turning its beak back, and then circle several times until Quinn had caught up. Only when the animal was confident that Quinn was still there would it then start off again. She couldn't even remember parts of the city she had been born and raised in, but she was flying through the streets so fast, she didn't have time to stop and look around. Her entire focus was on that bird.

It was the only other living thing in this vast expanse of city—in a place that should have held life—but instead only held emptiness and a hollow echo upon its walls. While she wasn't a proper gods-fearing woman, Quinn knew better than to ignore an omen sent.

She nearly tripped and fell face first into the street as a lamp hanging on the second roof to a nearby building began to glow. She slowed, whipping her head back. Night was falling in this dream world as lamps from every building and house began to illuminate. Nothing and no one had touched them. The fires merely flared up on their own—lighting up within the little paper structures as they swayed above the doorways.

A sharp cry sounded above her. Quinn jerked her head back and saw that the bird had returned for her. It cried once more, flapping its wings in animalistic outrage. Then it took off again.

And again, Quinn followed. Though, this time, she did

so at a slower pace. Did it want her to look around? To see what had become of Liph? She couldn't tell, seeing as the blasted thing was unable to speak.

Quinn glanced back to the ground, to the homes that she couldn't recall ever seeing before. It was far darker than any of the streets she had traversed in her old life. The buildings were closer together and run down, stains on the outsides of the wall. Windows hung open. Broken doorways led into barren places. Ice and snow collected on the roofs, hanging above each entrance. That same snow compacted on the sides of the street, turning into icy slush, but her feet had long since grown numb to the pain of the ice and the glass shards still lodged in her soles.

As she passed under a low hanging bridge connecting one building to another, Quinn slowed her steps even further as she spotted an open square. Cerulean eyes slowly assessed the area, her lips parting in confusion as her brows drew together. Quinn gaped at the statues lining the front of an ancient structure.

One was headless, while another had an arm missing, and all of them—save for one—was badly in need of a washing.

She glanced beyond them to the temple itself. Its build was N'skari in nature. The architecture simple and obviously aided by Maji hands, as was told by the markings on the pillars lining the front entrance. The roofs were sloped and the walls lower than most N'skari temples. All of that was pale compared to the state of disrepair it had fallen into. Quinn searched for sign as to why, her eyes drawn toward the statues of the gods once more as she stepped forward.

The bird circled overhead, descending to land upon the roof as it watched her read the bottom of each statue.

Beliphor, The God of Death.

Leviathan, The God of Moon and Shadows.

Tikkoh, The God of Fire.

Saltira, The Goddess of War.

Neiss, The God of Fear.

Quinn paused, looking up at the god of fear. His eyes, legend said, were as yellow as the sun. His hair made of snakes. His skin as hard as the stone that his likeness was carved from. Each statue presented them all as beautiful, but terrifying beings. She realized why this temple appeared abandoned. These were the dark gods. The gods that breathed out the darkness and set it upon the land. Fear. War. Shadows. Fire. Death. To the N'skari, they were not to be revered. They were to be feared.

Quinn's fingers trailed across the markings of their names, lifting her head as her eyes met those of Neiss. Did he know of her? she wondered silently. Did he watch from the realm of the divine? Quinn paused when her fingers hovered over the last name; the last and largest statue. With a sharp inhale, she brushed away a bit of snow and read.

"Mazzulah of the Dark Realm." Neither god nor goddess, and yet both in one. The only god cursed to live as man by day and woman by night.

As soon as she finished saying their names aloud, the doors to the temple before her cracked open. The dark bird cawed, diving down and disappearing through the entrance. Quinn took that as her invitation. She ascended the steps to the fallen temple—forgotten by many and hated by the light—left to rot in the depravity of Liph.

Just as her hand touched the door she was swept backwards, called by the waking realm. Quinn yelled, her nails digging into the stone doors, clutching for the temple's opening, but it was too late. A violent cry left her lips as she was pulled from her dream. No matter how hard she fought to stay, an invisible force grabbed ahold of her limbs and dragged her into the shadows. And even as Quinn struggled against an unseen energy, she could have sworn she heard someone calling her name.

A woman.

From inside *the temple.*

Quinn jerked upward with a curse, sweat beading on her brow and sliding into her hairline as she turned, seeking out whatever had awoken her. The hammock she'd been sleeping in swung awkwardly as she attempted to get out, catching and flinging her from its hold. Quinn hit the floor with a painfully audible thump.

Rubbing her head and getting to her feet, Quinn glanced around, but no one was there. Shouts and the clashing of metal above her head alerted her to the cause of the empty sleeping quarters.

Retrieving her staff and sliding Imogen's gift over her knuckles, Quinn hurried to the stairwell. It took her much longer than she would have liked to get to the top as she had to pause every few feet and grab onto the railing or risk falling all the way back down as the ship was tilting one way and then the next.

The glow of a morning horizon bloomed beneath the darkness of the night sky, letting her know that daylight was almost upon them as she reached the exit, popping her head out. Quinn's mouth gaped as a flash of white passed her by— silver hair tied at the nape of a man's neck as he attacked one of the crewmen.

Quickly as she could, Quinn scrambled the rest of the way up and took in her surroundings as she realized what was going on. A man cried out into the dawn. Someone was flung over the railing into the unforgiving waters below. Blood splashed the deck.

Just as she went to take a step forward, a body fell from above—one of the Ilvan mercenaries who had agreed to come with them—his neck cracked at an odd angle as he stared unseeing into the vast nothingness of the afterworld to which his soul had departed. With a scowl, Quinn stepped over the corpse.

The N'skari had come for them.

To be continued . . .

Quinn and Lazarus story continues in :
Twisted is the Crown
Dark Maji Book Three

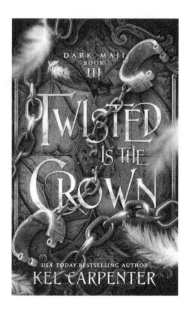

Also by Kel Carpenter

Ongoing Series:

—Adult Urban Fantasy—

Demons of New Chicago:

Touched by Fire (Book One)

Haunted by Shadows (Book Two)

Blood be Damned (Book Three)

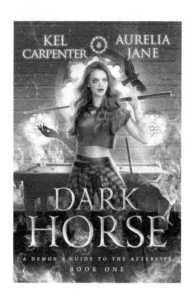

—Adult Reverse Harem Paranormal Romance—

A Demon's Guide to the Afterlife:

Dark Horse (Book One)

Completed Series:

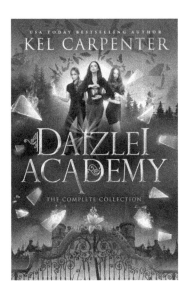

—Young Adult +/New Adult Urban Fantasy—

The Daizlei Academy Series:

Completed Series Boxset

—Adult Reverse Harem Urban Fantasy—

Queen of the Damned Series:

Complete Series Boxset

—New Adult Urban Fantasy—

The Grimm Brotherhood Series:

Complete Series Boxset

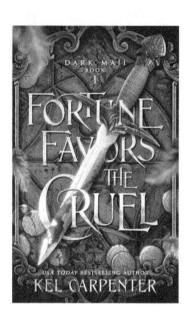

—Adult Dark Fantasy—

The Dark Maji Series:

Fortune Favors the Cruel (Book One)

Blessed be the Wicked (Book Two)

Twisted is the Crown (Book Three)

For King and Corruption (Book Four)

Long Live the Soulless (Book Five)

About Kel Carpenter

Kel Carpenter is a master of werdz. When she's not reading or writing, she's traveling the world, lovingly pestering her editor, and spending time with her husband and fur-babies. She is always on the search for good tacos and the best pizza. She resides in Bethesda, MD and desperately tries to avoid the traffic.

Join Kel's Readers Group!

CPSIA information can be obtained
at www.ICGtesting.com
Printed in the USA
BVHW031710010323
659501BV00015B/93